GLOCKS ON SATIN SHEETS 2

Adrian Dulan

**Lock Down Publications and Ca$h
Presents**
Glocks on Satin Sheets 2
A Novel by *Adrian Dulan*

2

Glocks on Satin Sheets 2

Lock Down Publications
P.O. Box 944
Stockbridge, Ga 30281

Visit our website @
www.lockdownpublications.com

Copyright 2020 Adrian Dulan
Glocks on Satin Sheets 2

Lock Down Publications
Like our page on Facebook: Lock Down Publications @
www.facebook.com/lockdownpublications.ldp
Cover design and layout by: **Dynasty Cover Me**
Book interior design by: **Shawn Walker**
Edited by: **Lashonda Johnson**

Adrian Dulan

Stay Connected with Us!

Text **LOCKDOWN** to 22828 to stay up-to-date with new releases, sneak peaks, contests and more…

Thank you.

Submission Guideline.

Submit the first three chapters of your completed manuscript to ldpsubmissions@gmail.com, subject line: Your book's title. The manuscript must be in a .doc file and sent as an attachment. Document should be in Times New Roman, double spaced and in size 12 font. Also, provide your synopsis and full contact information. If sending multiple submissions, they must each be in a separate email.

Have a story but no way to send it electronically? You can still submit to LDP/Ca$h Presents. Send in the first three chapters, written or typed, of your completed manuscript to:

LDP: Submissions Dept
P.O. Box 944
Stockbridge, Ga 30281

DO NOT send original manuscript. Must be a duplicate.

Provide your synopsis and a cover letter containing your full contact information.

Thanks for considering LDP and Ca$h Presents.

Adrian Dulan

About the Author

My name is Adrian Dulan. I was born on August 5, 1976. I'm 43 years old with five beautiful daughters and a handful of grandchildren. I'm currently incarcerated for Possession with Intent. I've been locked up since 2013 and I'm more than halfway finished with this journey. I enjoy writing, reading, and most importantly studying my Creator. I've taken a liking to the study of Memphite Theology and how some of the world's biggest religions started. Some of my goals for the near future is to get into writing movies, faith-based novels, thrillers, and horror. I went to school in Guthrie Oklahoma, as well as in Miami Beach, in Florida.

If you'd like to contact me you can hit me up on Facebook by looking up my name, or you can write to me at,

Adrian Dulan 11285010
Federal Correctional Institution
P.O. BOX 7000
Texarkana, TX 75505

I look forward to hearing from you soon.

Glocks on Satin Sheets 2

Acknowledgments

*All praise and glory to God. I love you and I thank you. I
am forever your humble servant. I also want to thank my
momma and daddy -- dad too. Get it? I'd like to thank Ca$h
and everyone else at Lock Down Publications for their work
putting this project together.*

*Ant, what up dawg? You thought I forgot? To Adrianna
Dulan, always know Daddy loves you. Ne'Airra McDaniel,
smile. Don't get it twisted, I love you and I appreciate y you
being a good role model for your little sister. Keep up the
good work.*

*To all the readers that continue to turn the pages of my
books and look forward to reading my new work, thank you.
Stay tuned—I'm going in!*

Adrian Dulan

Chapter 1

The End Of The Beginning

McCracken stood staring down at Puncho's lifeless body. The sight of his disfigured face was quite disturbing. Here laid the person that had shot and killed, Agent Jefferson but who had shot and killed him? Clearly, Poncho had been robbed of the money used for the bogus drug deal but why was he killed as well?

Unable to come up with a reasonable explanation, McCracken concluded his investigation stating that it appeared to be an inside job, fueled by greed.

"McCracken!" Stevens called out as he approached him from behind. "Do you think it'd be a good idea for me to go ahead and escort Agent Brown home for the evening? He's really starting to come apart over there. I figured it'd be best if we get him out of here as quickly as possible."

McCracken grudgingly looked away from the hideous sight before him. He peered back at the black suburban that sat just beyond the chain-linked fence. It was hard to imagine how much pain and frustration must've been building up inside Agent Brown. Stevens was right, it was probably a good idea to get him out of there.

"Before you take him in for the evening, I'd like a moment to have a word with him." McCracken headed towards a small opening in the fence that was used as a quick entrance into the apartment complex. He ducked low so as not to snag his jacket on some of the many jagged edges, he eased through the fence and made his way over to the truck. "How're you hanging in there?" he asked getting in on the driver's side and casually tossing his clipboard on the dash.

Agent Brown peered over at McCracken solemnly and said, "I let him down. Jefferson counted on me to be his back up and now he's dead because of me!" Brown began to weep uncontrollably. He slammed his fist into the dashboard and yelled, "I want the son of a bitch dead! Whoever is responsible for doing this, I want his fuckin' head!"

"Calm down. Calm down!" McCracken insisted while patting Brown on the shoulder and gently squeezing it. "You're being way too hard on yourself. Jefferson knew the possible consequences of this job when he took it. Don't blame yourself for something you didn't have control over. That could've just as easily been you. This thing was totally out of your control. There wasn't nothing you could've done to stop it."

"But there was something I could've done! I could've searched the damn kid. I could've watched him more closely. I could've done anything besides stand there and watch him shoot my partner to death!"

McCracken slowly shook his head and said, "I understand you think you could've done something, but you still need to calm down."

"I am fucking calm!"

"No, you're not. You're yelling and screaming at me thinking that's going to change something, but it's not. We all lost someone very important to us today. Don't you think for one second you're the only one who feels that pain."

Agent Brown cradled his head in his hands and cried, "So, what now? What in the hell am I supposed to do now? Agent Jefferson's shooter is dead his accomplice is somewhere out there with our fucking money. We don't have any leads, no suspects. What are we gonna do besides sit around taking pictures all damn night?"

McCracken peered over at Agent Brown with a stern look. He hated to be the bearer of bad news, but Agent Brown was in no condition to be working this investigation. "Let's say for starters, you go home and take the next couple of weeks off on vacation. You look like you need some time to rest, just long enough for you to get your head back in the game."

"Are you serious? My head's been in the game! Just because—"

10

"Sorry, son, I can't have you running around half-cocked, making decisions based on your emotions. Innocent people's lives are at stake. We've got too much on the line. We have some very promising evidence that should ultimately lead to Jefferson's killer's accomplice. But— we need to be sure and take the proper steps along the way." McCracken dug into his jacket and pulled out a plastic bag containing a cell phone.

"Ya' see this?" he asked while dangling the bag beside him for Brown to see. "We pulled this off the shooter. This phone contains the number to the phone that was contacting Agent Jefferson throughout the investigation. We believe, the number in this phone belongs to our guy. The shooter's accomplice. All we need to do is GPS the phone attached to that number and we've got him!" McCracken rolled the bag back up and stuffed it back into his pocket.

"Listen, I understand what's going on here," Brown stated matter of factly. "I've been part of this Agency for five long years. I know how things work around here. I can do this. Don't take me off the case when we're so close to bringing these sons of bitches down!"

"It's out of my hands," McCracken replied holding his hands in the air. "Your commanding officer will be over here in just a moment to take you back to headquarters."

"But, but, but— listen—"

"No, you listen, I'm going to advise that you take the next few weeks off to get yourself together. Those are the rules, that's how these things work." McCracken opened his door and slid out, just as it began to rain. He quickly retrieved his clipboard off the dashboard and stood shielding his head from the falling rain. "Take care of yourself, Brown. I wanna see you back in the field when it's time to bring the rest of these guys in."

Agent Brown cursed himself as McCracken slammed the door and shuffled back to the crime scene. There was no way he'd rest while his partner laid dead in the streets. No soon as Stevens escorted him back to headquarters, it was time to take justice into his own hands.

***

"What up. Grinders?" Lil Menace greeted Crazy Cuz, Big Crip, and C-Loc as he mobbed up on the porch at Big Crips house. "Being that I knew niggaz would be salty over shit that I've said, I stopped by so you could hear it straight from me. I 'on't want no misunderstandings. I need y'all to know that this is how I'm moving now."

Crazy Cuz was the first to laugh, prompting everyone else to join in. "This nigga must be high off that shit again?" he exclaimed. "He tryin' to put on like you bout 'dat, but 'erbody know tha' bizzness. You just running yo' muthafuckin' mouth, cuz."

Lil Menace smirked because of his response. He knew he'd be met with this type of hostility. The time for him to be looked at as the little homie had come and gone. It was time for him to be a man, now. It was time to set things in order like a gangsta. "I bet that mark ass nigga, I leftover in tha' 'jects know what tha' bizness is. Since you think I'm just flexin'. Why don't chu' ask him and let him be the one to tell you."

Big Crip may have been laughing along with everyone else, but he knew better than to take for granted what Lil Menace said. "What nigga are you talking about?" he inquired, smiling, yet only to make it appear that he was trying to be entertained.

"I'm talking about that bitch ass nigga you was tryin' to have a truce with," Menace spat. "I left cuz, dead and stankin' over in tha' projects earlier today. Twelve over there right now combing the area for evidence. But since some of you niggaz claim to know how I get down, then it goes without saying. No evidence. No Case. All I leave is dead bodies."

C-Loc bolted up out of his chair, openly challenging Lil Menace, and said, "Nigga, you don't get no props because you done fucked around and started a war. We was doin' fine wit' out all tha' bullshit. Why tha' fuck you always doin' dumb shit?"

Lil Menace sized C-Loc up as he inched dangerously closer to him. "Get tha fuck out of my face, cuz," he snarled. "I did what yo 'peace treaty lookin' ass wouldn't do. If a muthafucka ain't a Grinder, tha' fuck I look like sparing 'em? While everyone sitting around waiting on them Crimson Mafia niggas to get our hood back right, I said fuck it and went and got right on my own."

No one said a word. Before when Lil Menace spoke it was all fun and games. Now, he had everyone's undivided attention.

"I got enough paper stashed away to go buy at least four or S bricks," Lil Menace went on to say, "I been hittin' them niggaz so hard I figured it was time for us to start doing our own thang." He dug into his pocket, pulled out a cigarette, and lit it. He wanted to give everyone enough time to digest the juicy bit of information he'd just dropped on them.

C-Loc looked from Menace to Big Crip, then finally over at Crazy Cuz. "Y'all hear this, nigga? This fool must've got so damn high that he think he John Gotti or something. What muthafucka in their right mind, would ever think this broke ass nigga got some paper?" Everyone erupted into laughter causing Lil Menace's temper to boil.

He calmly took another puff from his cigarette and daringly blew it into C-Loc's face. "I've been listening to you niggaz talk shit ever since I got here," Lil Menace snarled. "From now on, y'all gon' have to watch how you comin' at me. Just because y'all tha big homies, don't mean you can disrespect me."

Crazy Cuz jumped to his feet sensing the sudden change in Lil Menace's attitude. Although he had every reason to be upset, Crazy Cuz still didn't feel it. "You need to pipe down wit' all tha' extras," he insisted. Ain't nothing but day one Grinders over here, cuz. All that cuff guy shit gon' getcha wig split."

Lil Menace chuckled softly and replied, "Somehow you done got me mixed up with somebody else. I bet not one nigga gon' touch me. Whatchu' bet?"

Crazy Cuz shoved him down the porch steps and took off his shirt. "You think you hard now, cause you done caught a body? I touched you, nigga, so do somethin'!"

Lil Menace calmly pulled out his trusty .40 cal and racked a bullet in the chamber. "What that Grinder life like, cuz?" To pull a strap on one of the S   homies was against the code.

The Steady Grinding Boyz honored fair ones amongst their own. Technically, when Lil Menace drew down on Crazy Cuz, he was open game.

"Oh, so you ready to die because I pushed you, nigga?" Crazy Cuz quipped.

"Because that's how this shit is about to play out." Lil Menace stood firm, glaring up at Crazy Cuz, then pointed his gun at him.

"I been ready to die," he spoke fearlessly. "Since you poppin' all that killa shit, gon' and getcha' gun— I'll wait."

Big Crip quickly stepped to the edge of the porch and pulled Crazy Cuz behind him. "Tha' fuck is yo' problem, cuz? You pullin' burners on tha' homies, yet you call yo' self a Grinder?"

Lil Menace ice grilled Big Crip. Gone was the little home that would tuck his tail when the big homie spoke up. All that remained was the fearless young goon that they'd raised him to be.

"Fuck that nigga, cuz!" Lil Menace remarked. "If that nigga ever put his hands on me again, I'll body his bitch ass, too."

Big Crip nodded, acknowledging that he understood, then said, "So, you just gon' keep pointin' that gun at me?"

Lil Menace sized C-Loc up, before allowing his signature gaze to fall upon Crazy Cuz. Once he was certain his message was clear, he reluctantly lowered his gun. "Now where was I before I was so rudely interrupted?" Menace pushed past Crazy

Cuz, intentionally nudging him with his shoulder.

Big Crip couldn't help but admire his young protege's performance. He stood fearless although his infraction warranted death. Although everyone, except for Big Crip, wanted to try Lil Menace they didn't. He kept a firm grip on his big black .40 cal so niggas knew to keep their attitudes in check.

Adrian Dulan

Chapter 2

I See Dead People

Mob awoke the next day to an excruciating headache. His head pounded away as if it had a heartbeat of its own. He slowly rolled to the edge of the bed where nausea threatened to explode from within. He quickly flung the covers back and rushed into the bathroom, straight to the toilet. "Errrrgggghhh!" He vomited into the commode.

Chunks of last night's meal splashed into the toilet before him. Mob closed his eyes, willing himself to try and control his breathing. Seemingly, the slightest whiff of the wrong thing would send him back into a vomiting fit. When he'd finally began to feel the tension in his gut subside, he opened his eyes, but quickly snapped them shut.

"It's not real. It's not real. It's not real!" he spoke softly to himself.

What he'd saw in the toilet was but a reminder of the ruthless villain that he'd been over the past several years. After all the people he'd killed, his mind had begun to play tricks on him. Mob slowly rose to his feet, swiping away beads of sweat from his brow. He walked over to the sink and peered intently at himself in the mirror.

"Tha fuck is wrong with me?" His six-foot, 187 pounds frame, was a far cry from the solid hunk of muscle that he was accustomed to being at. Even his sea sickening taper—fade didn't have the sharp edge that accentuated his handsome features.

When Mob turned on the water to rinse out his mouth, he had a vision. A dead woman cradling a child stood next to him. He knew them because he'd recently killed them. It was Derrick's wife and his son. Frustrated, yet startled, Mob stormed back into his bedroom and slammed the door in a panic-stricken state.

He took a partially smoked cigarette out of the ashtray and

lit it. The nicotine that coursed through his body was in fact, just what he needed. Now, that he was no longer haunted by visions of dead people, he focused on what needed to be dealt with. Considering everything that could possibly go wrong, undoubtedly going wrong inside the Crimson Mafia, he needed to have a level head.

The gentle buzz from his cell phone vibrating on the nightstand disturbed his train of thought. "Speak," Mob growled into the phone while taking his seat on the edge of the bed. The caller wasted no time getting straight to the point. They were willing to accept whatever terms necessary to get business back rolling. "Hold up, before you say too much," Mob spoke sternly to the caller. "We need to have this conversation face to face. You don't ever know who's listening in."

After a few brief moments and confirmation of a meeting place, the deal was sealed. Mob ended the call with a slight glimmer of hope for his crumbling organization. Now that the Steady Grinding Boyz were willing to put up the loot to purchase their packages, expansion was inevitable. Mob couldn't continue to maintain the Crimson Mafia without some help from outside resources.

***

2 Weeks Later

Young Sykes lay handcuffed to a hospital bed, several days after he'd awoke from a coma. For the life of him, he couldn't remember what had happened. The last thing he recalled was picking Slim up from the airport. He wondered had the car been shot up, which would explain the wreck and his bullet-riddled body. Millions of questions danced around in his head, but he'd never find out the truth as long as he had those handcuffs on.

"Mr. Ramsey," McCracken greeted him upon strolling into

Young Syke hospital room.

"Who is you?" Young Syke asked, eyeing the older white man suspiciously.

"Let's just say I'm a friend of a friend, shall we? I'm here to ask you a few questions about the night you were shot. Hopefully, that'll shed some light on why you're being arrested."

"Arrested? So, I'm being arrested because I got shot?"

"No, you're being arrested because you broke the law!"

Young Syke smirked and looked away. "I don't fuck with tha' police, fam," he snarled. "You might as well gon' and bounce before you waste too much of your day."

McCracken nodded and calmly slid his hands in his pockets. It took everything he was made of not to explode on Young Syke. "Are you sure I'm the one you don't wanna fuck with?" he asked. "Cause I'm the one with the power to make your life a living hell. Now if that's something that you can deal with, then fine! I'll just turn my ass around and walk right back out that door."

Young Syke glared up at McCracken, batting his eyes as if he could blink him away. "You ain't left yet?" he sassed.

"You listen here, you little dick suckin' son of a bitch! I'm gonna' bury you under the prison. Do you understand me? *Bury!* That goes for you, and that no good slick talkin'—"

"McCracken!" Timothy Liggans shouted from the doorway. "That's enough."

McCracken looked back to see who had spoken, then quickly turned his attention back to Young Syke. "This isn't over by a long shot, fucker! Don't you forget what I told you." McCracken blew him a kiss, then stormed out of the room.

"Do you mind telling me what in the hell that was about?" Timothy Liggans asked after closing Young Syke's hospital room door behind them.

McCracken released a loud sigh and stood staring up at the ceiling. "I don't know what that was about," he replied, apologetically. "I was mad, I overreacted. I wasn't thinking about what I was doing. I just hate to see these kids act like this is a game. Lives are being lost. Families are being destroyed because of people like them and the drugs they flood our streets with." McCracken turned as if to go back into Young Syke room, but stopped just short and took a deep breath.

"I think you need to calm down," Liggans insisted. "Why don't we have us a seat over there?" He gestured toward two empty chairs not far from where they stood. "Even though it appears we have a lot stacked against us, that still doesn't give you the right to break the law."

McCracken sat down next to Liggans, resting his elbows on his knees. He stared down at the floor dazed, struggling to come up with an explanation for his actions. "I know," he solemnly admitted. "There's just so much riding on this case. Sometimes I get caught up in my feelings and I just—react!"

Timothy Liggans shook. his head and said, "That's no excuse. You are a Federal Agent. You are expected to uphold the law and conduct yourself accordingly. Does that sound like the oath that you've taken?"

"It does, but-but-but—" he sighed and said, "I'm sorry."

Timothy Liggans smiled and patted him on the shoulder. "No need to continue to harp on the past. Tell me, have you come up with a plan to get Mr. Ramsey to lead us to our shooter's accomplice?"

McCracken peered over at him seemingly confused. "I didn't know we were going to use him. Ramsey was here whenever the shooting took place. Not to mention, he probably has no idea what's been going on. I assumed we'd just use Slim. Now that the shooter's accomplice ditched the phone. We have to come at him with everything we've got. I figure that's the only way we can get him to talk."

Liggans appeared to be in deep thought. "Maybe. Maybe not," he said. "What if we let Mr. Ramsey walk right out of here like he's a free man? We already know he and his crew are close-knit it wouldn't be long before he'd lead us right to where we need to be. Mind you, we already have him on the selling of two kilos. That gives us the freedom to search whenever we feel the time is right. All you need to do is put eyes on his location. As long as you can do that, we've got 'em!"

"But what if that plan doesn't work? What then? You're already all over me about the havoc the Crimson Mafia is wrecking on the city. I don't need this to end up backfiring on me."

Liggans chuckled. "This was my idea, remember? If my plan doesn't work, then it's on me. I'm willing to pull out all the stops, but you just make sure you don't make me look like an ass for doing it."

McCracken smiled broadly. "I can do that," he said while slightly laughing. "As long as you've got my back, then I definitely can do that."

"Good. Now, go in there and tell Mr. Ramsey there has been some kind of terrible misunderstanding. Be sure and make it sound believable. We don't need him suspecting us of anything."

Adrian Dulan

Chapter 3

The Beginning

1 Year Later

McCracken stood gazing down into the city streets from his 12th-floor office. The downtown Oklahoma City streets were buzzing with excitement. It had been a long tiresome day at the Federal Bureau of Investigations. McCracken and his team scoured through hours of countless wiretaps. Luckily, the dreadfully tedious work had paid off. Agents were now moments from revealing the identity or yet another major drug supplier.

"This woman—" McCracken began by saying while still peering down into the city streets. "—I wonder how is it that De'Marco Johnson, or should I say, Lil Menace even met someone like this in the first place. I mean, the guy is a freakin' gang banger slash stickup kid for crying out loud. Now, not even a year since his last run-in with the law, he's an official Crimson Mafia member buying kilos?"

Stevens stirred in his chair. "It does seem kind of strange if that's what you're asking me," he admitted. "But I believe, the bigger question is, why is everything going so smoothly? With all this new dope flooding the streets, it's crazy that no one has been killed yet."

McCracken turned and peered back over his shoulder, as uncertainty crept into his eyes. He took ahold of his necktie and loosened it, then walked over to his desk. "What if the Crimson Mafia doesn't know that Mr. Johnson is doing this?" he asked and took a seat. "What if all this under the table dealing is so that Lil Menace and his crew can take over the drug trade? Let's keep in mind, these two groups were at each other's throat just over a year ago. Who's to say that the Steady Grinding Boyz aren't trying to make their move to control the drug trade?"

Adrian Dulan

Stevens appeared to give it some thought, but quickly dismissed the idea with a half-hearted chuckle. "I think you're reaching," he said and looked at McCracken skeptically. "It's been a long day. Let's just take whatever we have and call it quits for now."

McCracken smirked and rolled his eyes. "I'm reaching now? You know just as well as I do, I'm generally right when I get a hunch about something."

"Yeah, yeah, I hear you. But, we have more than enough evidence that we should be focused on. We've still yet to find Young Syke since his release from the hospital. Agent Brown is still undercover trying to get us as close to whoever is running the Crimson Mafia. And that's not to mention that Derrick Walker is still unwilling to cooperate. Now, I don't know about you, but I just worked up an appetite thinking about all of the work that's ahead of us." Stevens stood and playfully patted his bulging stomach. "I think Margaret is making your favorite tonight."

McCracken shook his head in defeat. "Now why did ya have to go there? Taco soup sure does sound really good right about now. Do you think she'll blend us up a few of those tasty Margaritas?"

Stevens snatched up his jacket off the back of his chair and said, "There's only one way to find out. I'll meet you at the car."

Freddy B's head swayed back and forth as unconsciousness threatened to overcome him. He'd been strapped to a chair, hands behind his back and feet tied to the legs of the chair. To allow himself to slip away into unconsciousness, might mean he'd never wake up again.

"Wait!" he slurred, as Young Syke held his fist high ready to deliver yet another bone-crushing blow. "I'll tell you whatever you need to know. Just please— no more."

Young Syke smiled triumphantly while peering down at the leader of the Hill Side Courtz. Although, once a member of the notorious Crimson Mafia, greed and karma had played its

24

role bringing this young boss to his demise. "Where tha fuck is tha money you owe us?" Young Syke snarled. "And where did you get this dope from?" Syke snatched up a plastic bag containing a kilo of dope off the table. He held the bag inches from Freddy B's face forcing him to look at it.

Freddy B shook his head in disgust and peered down at the floor. The truth would surely cost him his life. He was damned if he told him, and damned if he didn't. "I already told you," he solemnly spoke. "I got a plug outta Dallas. I been flipping the work that you front me, then—"

Wham!

Syke's hit him so hard that he nearly knocked over the chair. "Keep playing with me," he snarled. "I can do this shit all night. It's been new dope floodin' the city for the past eight months. You didn't think we'd notice that someone was trying to move in on our territory?"

Freddy B laid his head on the back of the chair and stare up into the ceiling. If he continued to hold out on Young Syke the interrogation could easily go on forever. "If I tell you what you wanna know, they'll kill me."

Syke's grabbed him by the hair and yanked his head back so that they stare eye to eye. "I see you still wanna play games, don't you? While you worried about what somebody else is gonna do, I'm 'bout to kill yo' stupid ass, right now!" Syke's scanned the living room that he and three other goons had literally ripped apart. Finding nothing he deemed suitable to inflict the type of pain he was ready to impose, he ordered Baby Jerk to get a butcher knife from the kitchen. "This is your last chance, fam-o. Either tell me what tha fuck I wanna know or I'ma empty out your guts."

Freddy B's eyes roamed over each man standing in the room until he'd finally saw the person he was looking for. He knew him. He could feel his ice-cold gaze warning him not to say a word. But the only reasonable option he had was to talk. Hopefully, Syke would spare him if he did. "Alright, listen—" he spoke softly as Baby Jerk shuffled back into the room carrying a butcher knife. "I'll tell you whatever you wanna know. But. give me your word that you won't kill me."

Young Syke's patience was wearing thin. He peered over at his comrades while holding the knife and hammered down into Freddy B's leg.

"Aaaahhh!" he howled in pain.

Syke twisted the handle, sawing, grinding. severing the muscles in his leg until the knife stopped on the chair. "You like that? I tol' you I can do this shit all night long. So, what it's gon' be? You can either tell me what I wanna know or next time I'll chop your fuckin' dick off!"

Freddy B's lip quivered as he tried to stifle another outcry. The pain was excruciating, but it could only get worse. There'd be no second chances. He knew what he had to do. "Just—just promise me you'll let me live."

Young Syke glared at him and started to pull the knife out of Freddy B's leg. "You still think I'm fuckin' around, don't chu'?"

Freddy B groaned, fighting with everything in him not to scream He peered up at Young Syke and said, "His-his-his name is Mena—"

Boom!

The sound of a Desert Eagle at close range was enough to make everyone winch while covering their ears. "Tha' fuck is you doing?" Young Syke asked. "You killed the nigga before he told us anything."

4 Lyfe stood glaring down the barrel of his gun. The thought to squeeze again had undoubtedly crossed his mind, but the job was done. There was no way Freddy B could survive a shot to the head at close range. "I got tired of listening to this nigga, spin you," he explained. "We got what we came here for. Let's just take whatever else we can find and leave."

Young Syke looked at Freddy B and almost gagged. His head hung down to his chest as white clumps oozed down the side of his face. Although Freddy B had been sentenced to die long before the Goon Squad had arrived, their objective was simple. Find the dope and money and force Freddy B to give up his connect.

"Who tha fuck told you that you was making decisions?" Young Syke barked. "The last I recall, you were told to do what tha' fuck I tol' you." 4 Lyfe   gritted on Syke and gave him a thorough once over. "If you got something on your chest, just say it! All that lookin' brazy ain't gon' do shit but get yo' face caved in like this niggaz shit."

Block Monsta and Baby Jerk came alongside Young Syke awaiting his command.

"I fucked up," 4 Lyfe frowned. "You know I ain't got no problems with you. It's Goon Squad ova everythang. You looking too deep into this, fam. I wanted him to give us the connect just as bad as you did."

Young Syke eyed 4 Lyfe sternly. There was no doubt in anyone's mind as to how he felt about an East-sider. But, being that Mob had opened business ties with them. Syke was forced to deal with them. "I'll tell you what. Since you was tha brilliant muthafucka' that decided to kill that nigga. I'ma leave it up to you to explain that shit to Mob. If that nigga ain't trippin'. then what tha' fuck I look like trippin'?"

While everyone went to work gathering things that they'd been sent to get, Young Syke watched 4 Lyfe's every move. It wasn't a coincidence that he killed Freddy B before he spoke. Hopefully, Mob would see the error in allowing an enemy to become part of the family.

Adrian Dulan

Chapter 4

We Started From Nothing

Young Syke whipped his silver Chevy Impala into the body shop known as Candy Coated. Candy Coated was a small shop located on the outskirts of Oklahoma City. Its sole purpose was to be used as a meeting place for the Crimson Mafia. Now that the Feds were seemingly lurking around every corner. Mob had to improvise when it came to the functions of this new facility. Candy Coated became the new headquarters for the Crimson Mafia. Shipments were delivered there, broke down, and stored there until they were transported to the main stash spot.

Mob had somehow managed to establish the perfect cover for their new operation. Paint and bodywork was being done by appointment only, while they illuminated the worry of stragglers stumbling across the spot by building a huge metal fence around the property. Not only could no one see inside but Candy Coated was on a dead-end street. No other businesses were anywhere near the property for at least four blocks.

After spending a few moments to get his thoughts together. Syke cut the car off and hopped out. "I want you niggaz to fall back and wait for me in the back," he ordered the squad. Syke scooped up the duffel bag containing the work out of the trunk. "Y'all already know this nigga fuck around and go ape shit about how thangs fell down." Young Syke glared at 4 Lyfe mockingly. He was certain that he'd be crucified for what he'd done.

Young Syke took to a flight of stairs that led up to Mob's second-floor office. Once there, he gently tapped on the door and went in.

"What do you mean, tha price gotta change?" Mob spoke sternly into the phone. "We been coppin' all this time at that price. I ain't fixin' to let you play me like that, damu. Tha price stays tha' same!"

Young Syke could hardly stand to hear Mob going hard on the connect like that. Either there was about to be a severe drought or the Goon Squad was about to put in some work.

"Damn it." Mob slammed the phone down and sat up to his desk. "Them bitch ass niggaz must don't know who they dealing with. I'll murder all them muthafuckas. I don't give a fuck who they is."

Syke shook his head, not wanting to see Mob so frustrated. When tempers started to flare, his understanding was at a minimum. "Eaz up fam-o. I brought you a gift from ya boy, Freddy B. Everything is good. We just gotta figure out how we gon' weather the storm." Syke sat the duffle bag on top of Mob's desk. Surely, he thought Mob would be excited to see what he had in the bag.

Surprisingly—he wasn't. "*Weather the storm*?" Mob repeated mockingly. "Have you forgot that we hot as fish grease? Have you forgot we struggling to get by? We in this bitch frontin' like we gettin' money. Business ain't been right since Slim brought that snake ass bitch, April into tha' fold."

Young Syke nodded that he understood and plopped down on a sofa. The reality of their situation was all a product of their own doing. If they expected to find their way back to the top of the game, it'd be up to them to do it.

"You're right, I feel you, fam-o. We hot as fish grease but that's part of it. Things ain't gon be like they were when Slim was runnin' tha show. You a different kinda breed, fam-o. You got niggaz shook! You used to getting what you want by applying a different kind of pressure."

Mob leaned back in his chair with a slight smirk and said, "You think you got all the answers, don't you?"

Young Syke shrugged. "Tha shit speaks for itself. You gotta flip the script and let somebody else take the wheel. Let the streets think it ain't what it is."

Mob took a moment to digest that information. This was exactly the type of feedback he'd been needing. Since Slim was gone and him no longer communicating with the Crimson Mafia, Young Syke had become the only person he could talk to.

"So, what is it that you're suggesting?" Mob inquired. "The connect trippin' because our re-up isn't the same. Our clientele done dwindled down to nothing, because niggaz is spooked. The whole city is on fire. I mean, *what*?"

Young Syke brushed his hand over his chin looking as if he were in deep thought. He had millions of ideas dancing around in his head, but none of them made any sense, except for one. "What if we take over the Hill Side Courtz?"

He finally replied, "Everybody knows the Courtz is rollin'. We can start breakin' down bricks rock for rock. That'll give us a chance to get our money right."

Mob sat up to his desk appearing to be intrigued. "You might be on somethin'," he admitted. But if Freddy B is still alive that's like going to war with ourselves."

Young Syke hopped up and went to show Mob the contents inside the duffle bag. Opposed to telling him about what 4 Lyfe had done, he'd decided to keep quiet. This might prove to be his only opportunity to move up in ranks. He wouldn't dare lead Mob to believe that he couldn't handle his position.

"Freddy B is dead," Young Syke stated as a matter of factly. "Fam-o would rather get his brains blown out than give up his plug. Dude was loyal until the death of him. He didn't say nothing!" Syke removed one of the Ziplock bags from the duffle bag. Big bold letters that read, *T.O.* instantly grabbed Mob's attention.

"Whoever this, T.O. person is, don't give a fuck!" Mob exclaimed. "They slowly taking over our territory. Every time I turn around, I'm hearing something about this muthafucka. I wonder who in tha fuck it could be?" Mob fell silent while he carefully plotted on his next move. Although what Young Syke had presented made perfect sense, there were still too many unanswered questions. "Whatever you've gotta do to take over

31

tha Courtz, do it!" Mob went on to say. "It's time for us to flush out this, T.O. muthafucka, and get to the bottom of this. Since you talkin' that boss shit like you ready to take the wheel, start by making this mission work. Then we'll see if you've got what it takes."

Chapter 5

The Baddest Bitch

Club Timers, was the new hot spot for the grown and sexy to go out and get their groove on. Young adults ages 25 and up, flooded the fancy new spot just to get their party on with some of Oklahoma's a.k.a O City finest. R&B legends like Jagged Edge, Avant, Tank, and many others, graced the stage of the small establishment.

Big Bruce a 6'4, 320-pound bouncer, had been summoned to work that weekend. Although he was still a full-time bouncer at Club Kavey, Big Bruce still offered his services for some of Club Timers most elite. R&B singers and hood superstars alike might opt to hire the 6-foot-4 silverback to decorate their entourage. But that night, that option wasn't a luxury on the table. That night, Big Bruce had been asked to work the V.I.P for one of the baddest bitches to touch the Oklahoma City streets.

Bobbing and weaving through the dimly lit room, Big Bruce had finally made it to the V.I.P entrance in the back and stepped outside to do a perimeter check. Certain V.I.P guests required an extra heightened level of security. Shady business deals had led to bloody street wars, so that night—Big Bruce wasn't taking any chances. His security staff was definitely on point, so foolishness would not be tolerated.

The sound of *Jeezy's Fake Love* seeped out of the window of a jet-black Maserati as it crawled into the parking lot. The mere sight of the car was enough to put the entire parking lot on chill as it came to a stop right in front of the V.I.P entrance. Big Bruce being unaware as to who the occupants of the vehicle were, flashed his flashlight alerting other security guards to assist him. Moments later, the driver's door slowly opened revealing the intoxicating cherry red insides of perfection. Big Bruce bent down, peering inside as a gorgeous woman emerged from the car.

"Ms. Jordan," Big Bruce greeted April as she took his hand and got out.

Her all-white Altuzarra suit accompanied by Christian Louboutin Bandy pumps screamed top notch. While her small entourage of two ratchets exiting the passenger side front and rear- announced her boss status.

"I see you still up to doing tha same thing," April said as she sashayed right past him. "All that money you be raking in it shouldn't be nothing to have someone else to do the dirty work."

Big Bruce opened the door and led the way inside the club. Jill Scott's angelic voice filled the air. Her neo-soul, instant classic *Cross My Mind* echoed off the club walls. Partygoers looked on in awe, admiring the beautiful woman that commanded their attention. Her long, blue hair that flowed effortlessly over her shoulders was enough to shut a simple bitch down. The eminent presence of the baddest bitch was in the building and wasn't a damn thing anyone could do about it.

"Do you need anything before I take post?" Big Bruce inquired as April and her guests were seated.

"Yeah, if you see Big Crip or Lil Menace send them over here," April replied while digging through her Channel clutch for a mirror.

Big Bruce frowned. "Them Eastside niggaz, ain't nothin' but trouble. You sure you want that kind of heat hangin' around?"

April leaned in closer and patted the back of his hand. "I'm the hottest thing in the streets. You should already know this is about business. They've been expecting me."

Big Bruce chuckled, assuming that the business that she was referring to was the young ladies that were with her. Little did he know, April had become a bigger boss than he'd ever imagined.

April placed her mirror back inside her clutch and slid it on the table. Leaning back against the soft leather in the booth, she watched as Big Bruce hurried off to do as she'd requested. It felt good to be back home and in the position of power that she was now in. Considering all the drama happening in and around her life, it's amazing to know that things had turned out for the better. But was it worth it?

April signaled for the waitress to assist them in opening a bottle of champagne. After filling three small flutes, April lifted her glass to propose a toast. "To the Baddest bitches," she said, clinging her glass against her guest's flutes. As April sat her glass down and began admiring the sparkling diamonds that adorn her hand, the answer to the question she'd been pondering was perfectly clear. "You damn right, it was worth it!"

A little more than a year ago, April laid helplessly bleeding to death on a barn floor. The precious fluid that connected her life to the world as we know, pooled around her body. Cold shackles were clamped around her ankles and wrists to ensure that the light that once burned inside of her, would never burn again. The last thing she remembered from that terrifying moment in time, was her demented ex-boyfriend towering above her with a hideous smile.

"Kill her!" he barked.

Slim's voice echoed in April's mind, as his goons beat her into oblivion. The bone-crushing blows that the bats yielded proved not to be enough. Slim ordered his vicious attack dogs to assist in finishing her off. Unconsciousness swept over April like a blanket of protection. Her mind plummeted into a deep dark place where her tormentors couldn't reach her. Luckily, Federal Agents stormed the property, saving her. Slim and several of his men were arrested and booked in jail without bond.

Agents quickly secreted April away and made it to appear that she'd been murdered, with still no arrest for the blotched hit on Derrick, Federal Prosecutors couldn't afford to take a risk with their only star witness.

April awoke days later from what she could only hon was

a terrible nightmare. But as her eyes began to adjust to the sunlight raining down into her room, such wishful thinking was quickly abandoned. Bandages stretched over the length of her body. The mere sight of the extensive damage sent April into a raging fit. Doctors fought tirelessly to subdue her. Her broken bones had still yet to heal, and her stitches could easily rip!

Although badly injured and forced to live under the watchful eye of the Federal Government, she'd vowed to remain courageous in her pursuit of happiness.

April soon began calculating how much it'd take for a down payment on a new life. Being that the lavish lifestyle she was accustomed to could be bought with a price she knew she had to figure out something. April made a few calls to a handful of people that she could trust. If by chance she was able to move the 3 kilos she had hidden, sell her condo, and get rid of her luxury cars, she'd be right back to where she'd started. A quarter of a million dollars richer.

"What that Grinder life like, cuz?" Lil Menace announced as he mobbed into V.I.P with an entourage of Steady Grinding Boyz in tow. "What took you so long to get here?"

April giggled softly as Lil Menace slid in the booth and gave her a hug. Now that the Crimson Mafia had dwindled down to just a few members, April had made a team of their opposition. As long as everyone genuinely despised each other, who would dare reveal that she had a hand in all of the madness?

"*What took me so long*?" April repeated, sarcastically. "I been here for thirty minutes. You asked me to be here and celebrate your birthday, but cho' badass ain't nowhere to be found!"

Lil Menace ran his hand over his face, flashing his new jewelry. "You must've really been lookin' for ya' boy, huh? Had I known you was feelin' a nigga like this, I'd have rented a room so you and me can kick it."

April burst into laughter showing no regard to his antics.

Regardless of how funny Lil Menace may have appeared, he meant every word that came out of his mouth. "Boy, you is not ready for none of this pussy," April replied still laughing. "Instead of trying to push up on something that you can never have, you might need to figure out what you're going to do with all of this."

April's guests slid out of the booth and went to stand in front of Lil Menace. One wore a long white Nicole Miller wrap around dress with Manolo pumps, while the other was draped in an all-white tank top dress with the sides cut out.

"Damn! All this pussy for me?" Menace said eyeing the women lustfully. "I mean, I know today is my c—day, but—"

April winked and said, "Happy birthday, crazy man. I just hope that you know what to do with all of this."

April slid out of the booth and sauntered over to the railing that encircled the V.I.P section. From her elevated view, she could see everything going on around her. People talked, some danced, doing the ordinary things that people do when they went out to have a good time. As she stood enjoying the soulful sounds of *Jacquees All You Need* a man standing by the bar caught her attention. His menacing gaze seemed to be calculating her every move. When she walked, his eyes roamed. When she stopped, his eyes stopped, with everything April had stacked against her, she couldn't afford to get caught slipping.

"Big Bruce, who's that man standing over next at the bar?" she asked, but in the split second that she'd looked away the man had vanished.

"Who's who?" Big Bruce inquired. "I 'on't see nothing but tha regulars. I see a few new niggaz, but no one you should be uptight about."

April scanned the bar once again, hoping to catch a glimpse of the man. Something about the way he looked, his expression, his demeanor, made finding him that much more urgent. Just as April had finally given up, she spotted him. "There he is, by the back doo—" Recognition of who he was hit her like a freight train.

Even after everything that had transpired since the last time they were together, April still had deep feelings for him.

"April, is that him?" Big Bruce snapped staring in the same direction as April. *"April!"* Finally fed up with the awkward moment of silence, Big Bruce sprang into action. He quickly signaled for more security and instantly gave chase.

"Bruce, wait!" April yelled after him, but it was already too late.

Big Bruce plowed into the crowd with a small team of security hot on his heels. April cursed herself for possible being the reason to cause Derrick more pain. She couldn't stand the idea of something else happening to him. By the time she'd managed to wrestle her way through the crowd, the door was locked. No one was going anywhere.

Chapter 6

So Much Pain

Dark clouds hovered high above as Derrick drove through the Heaven's Gates Cemetery. Every other Sunday, he'd make time to visit with his wife and son who were buried there. Sometimes, Derrick would go visit and just ramble on for hours about how things could've been had the situation been different. Often, he'd come to pour out the mounds of resentment that weighed heavily on his heart. Today, like so many times before, regret was what plagued his conscious. But unlike any time before, those feelings had been awakened by the very things that had landed him there in the first place.

"They lied to me," he spoke angrily to no one in particular. "They lied to me and said that she was dead!" Derrick shut off his car and sat gazing aimlessly into the cemetery. He peered up into the sky only imaging, what if God could see him now. All his hate, pain, and frustration, laid bare for all to see.

Regardless of someone being buried not even 20 yards away, his heartfelt screams could be heard all throughout the cemetery.

Wish You Were Here by *Jamie Foxx*, whispered through Derricks speakers. He envisioned finding his wife and son waiting there at Heaven's Gates for him. He fought eagerly to rid his mind of such wishful thinking, but he was rendered a slave to his thoughts and a victim of longing. He couldn't wait until the blessed day came when he too would be laid to rest.

The auxiliary power on his car finally shut off. Derrick opened the door and stumbled out looking a complete wreck. His dark, denim jeans sagged well below his waist revealing a black 9mm resting snug against his waistline. The tight-fitting, v-neck t-shirt he wore was now loose. He'd been in it for the past couple of days. Derrick fell to his knees digging his fresh Timbs into the soil beneath him. Just as he released another flurry of screams into the heavens above, the clouds opened up

Adrian Dulan

releasing a flurry of its own. Light raindrops fell to the ground covering it, and the man that had just about given up on life.

"Derrick!" A man shouted as he moved with haste, approaching from behind. "Don't let go like this, be strong!"

Derrick continued to cry, unaware that someone had spoken to him. His face was laying on his wife and son's grave as he welled at the top of his lungs. But when the man placed his jacket over his shoulders to provide him protection from the freezing rain, Derrick snapped, "Tha' hell are you doing?" He shoved the man off him. He quickly drew his gun, yet, struggled to get off his knees.

"Calm down, Derrick. It's me, Deacon Jenkins. We heard you over here crying and came by to check on you."

Derrick eyed him sternly, as well as the man that walked up next to him. He knew them. They were men from the church.

"Sorry," Derrick solemnly stated. "I didn't hear either of you when you walked up." He swiped away the dirt on his jeans and stood up. His dreadlocks hung freely practically covering his face.

"I can't believe what I'm seeing, right now," Pastor Johnson spoke sincerely. "You've done a complete three-sixty, since the last time I spoke with you."

Derrick tucked his gun in the small of his back, staggered, then brushed his locks behind his ear. "The last time you and I talked, the wounds were still fresh," Derrick explained. "I don't know how you expected me to turn out. Sorry to disappoint you *pastor*, but it is what it is."

Pastor Johnson shook his head in utter disappointment. It saddened him to see Derrick in such bad shape. He'd known him since he was a child. "Is that the mark that you've chosen to wear?" The Pastor asked. "Packing guns isn't you. Stumbling around drunk isn't you. You know, I'm almost afraid to say it but—"

"Say what?"

"Nothing about you reminds me of the person you used to

40

be."

Derrick chuckled. "I should've known that was coming."

"Okay, I'll accept that. You should've, your mother and father didn't raise you to be carrying on like this."

"Out of respect, I'm not gon' even respond to that."

"Good! So, maybe you can tell me if that's the mark that you've chosen to wear?"

Derrick glanced down at his attire and said, "I don't know what in tha hell you're talking about. How 'bout you and this brotha right here just let me be. I came here to spend time with my family, not stand here and play these games in tha fucking rain."

The Pastor held up both hands as he and Deacon Jenkins turned to leave, and said, "The mark of the beast can be seen by your actions. It is a thought process of evil that starts in your head. I can see the mark because I see the things you do. God's children are identified by the good that they do. But Satans—" He shook one finger vigorously in the air as he neared the church van. "Satans servants have decided to take vengeance into their own hands. Now tell me Derrick—is that you?" The jewels he'd just dropped on him were too heavy for Derrick's clouded mind.

He stood stewing in anger, frustrated that his visit had been disturbed. Had he not known the men that had come to comfort him, there was no telling what he might have done.

Later That Night

Derrick laid on his sofa pondering things that had transpired over the weekend. But no matter how hard he tried to focus thoughts of April kept distracting him. He sat up on his sofa and cradled his head in the palm of his hands. He needed to focus. His mind began to wander back and forth between April and the people that he'd seen at the club surrounding her. Some of the people wore a ton of jewelry. The chains draped around their necks all bore diamond-encrusted plates that read: *SBG, APRIL*.

The infamous crew that controlled the city was none other than the Crimson Mafia. How some other gang was allowed to flaunt as if they controlled the streets had him baffled, he thought back to one of the many conversations he'd with McCracken.

He'd said, *"If those guys want you dead, then you're dead! They supply other crews and organizations that'll happily kill you if given the opportunity. Your safest bet is to join the Witness Protection Program. That's it!"*

McCracken's last words could've easily been mistaken for a threat, or a challenge. Derrick may not have been a gangster, or street savvy enough to infiltrate a crew such as the Crimson Mafia, but he was willing to do what it takes. Whatever he had to become in order for revenge, he was willing to be.

Derrick went to wash his face to rid himself of his twisted thoughts. But the ugly scars that covered his cheek was but a reminder of a nightmare that could never be forgotten. He traced his fingers over the thin lines left because of the reconstructive surgery. Doctors had done an impeccable job, yet Derrick could still see the difference. Fake teeth had been inserted where his own teeth had been knocked out. A metal plate was used to help reconstruct his jawbone. In his eyes, he was a hideous sight to behold. He was nothing more than a carbon copy of the man he used to be.

By the time Derrick retired to bed that night, three capital letters stood at the center of his thoughts, *SGB*. What did it mean? Who were they? If the SGB was a notable presence in the game, were they connected to the Crimson Mafia?

Chapter 7

Let's Take It Back

Crickets sang their late-night anthem as Mob strolled up to his porch. He quickly unlocked the door and hurried inside but was met by darkness.

"Yo', Syke!" he called out. "You up in here?" Mob flicked on the light switch only to find that the electric was off. He peered intently into the darkness waiting on Syke's response, but when none came, he immediately went on alert.

"He wants to see the light," someone spoke in the darkness. "He wants to see it, so let him see it!"

Mob instantly reached for his strap, but it was gone! He spun around and tried to open the front door, but someone came crashing into him.

The pressure of a massive forearm bearing down on the back of his neck sent him into a panic. At any moment he expected to hear his neck snap in two, but instead, a man snarled in his ear, "What took you so long to get here?" His breath smelled like death. Mob had to focus to suppress the nausea that now threatened to overcome him.

The man bore down harder causing Mob to see spots. He gritted his teeth in an attempt to keep from screaming, but the pain was unbearable, he screamed, "Ahhhh!"

Mob awoke to Young Syke shaking him vigorously. "Wake up, dawg! Wake up!"

Mob snatched his arm away from Young Syke and bolted up in his bed. "What tha fuck just happened?"

Young Syke peered down at him with a look of concern and replied, "You had a bad dream, fam-o. Ain't nobody here but you, me, and this muthafuckin' hammer." Young Syke lifted his gun hoping that the sight of it would provide Mob with some sort of comfort. "I heard you screaming from all the way downstairs That shit sounded like someone was up in here tryin' to get at you."

Mob sighed, frustrated. His eyes darted around the room as he slowly began to feel safe. "I keep havin' these fucked up dreams," he explained. "One minute I'm sleeping fine, and everything is cool, then the next- I'm running for my life. I keep dreamin' that muthafuckas that I already killed, are out to get me."

Young Syke nodded in understanding, having a good idea what was going on. "That shit you going through comes with the game, fam-o. We out there knockin' niggaz heads off, and you don't think that comes with a price?" Syke lifted his shirt to reveal old bullet wounds that covered his body, and said, "Somebody tried to rock ya' boy to sleep, but you in here complaining about some nightmares."

Mob shook his head in disappointment, suddenly realizing he may have overreacted. He laid back on his pillow and watched as Young Syke left his room. For the first time since Syke was released from the hospital, he was glad he'd told Syke to move in. Regardless of how nonsocial he'd become, Mob needed someone around that could help him cope with the demons he'd been battling.

"Thanks for being there when I needed you," Mob said as he descended the steps into his living room.

Young Syke sat in front of the big screen, pounding away on a game controller. He spared a peek over his shoulder then continued playing his game. "A lotta niggaz would've just let me look like a fool, then *dirty mac* me behind my back."

Young Syke paused the game and replied, "That ain't me, fam-o, I don't talk bad about a man behind his back. I treat a nigga like they treat me. You looked out for me by lettin' me be here, so I'm lookin' out for you."

Mob chuckled and went to sit down on the sofa. "That's why I fuck with you, damu. You're mature beyond your age. Plus, I can always count on you to handle that bizness." While Young Syke continued playing his game, Mob sparked up a blunt out of the ashtray. He'd been upstairs planning how their day would begin, so it was time to start putting things in order. "I need you and a couple of tha homies to put things in motion over in the Hill Side Courtz," he continued. "We can't let another day slip past without somehow benefiting from that situation."

Syke paused the game and peered back once again. "But what about a spot?" he inquired. "We ain't gotta place to chill at. We'll be like sittin' ducks waitin' on twelve to lock us up."

"It's always a smoker that's willing to let you open up shop. I'll place a few calls and find a place for you niggaz to post up at. All you gotta do is get some runners together so they can put the word out. Once them fiends know where to find them boulders, it's a *wrap*! Can't nobody compete with us, cause ain't nobody got work like us."

Young Syke rubbed his palms together already envisioning all the money they'd be making. His whole life prior to becoming a member of the Goon Squad consisted of getting his money off the curve. To take it back to that way of survival was something he could deal with.

"What time do you want us to come back so we can meet up with the plug?" he inquired.

Mob's attitude seeming switched gears at the mention of their connect. "Fuck them niggaz, bleed. I got other things that need my undivided attention. We got muthafuckas floodin' the streets with dope that's not ours, and you can rest assure that it's someone we fuck with."

Young Syke appeared perplexed. "But how you know that?"

"Because they know who all our clientele is. We damn near pushin' the same kind of work it's just got a different stamp on it."

"I bet it's them Eastside niggaz, fam-o. If we could somehow watch them niggaz more closely, I bet they're the ones behind it."

Mob dismissed his assumption with the swat of his hand. "Use ya head, dawg. We tha ones supplying them fools. How they gon' be bringing in bricks, but they steadily beatin' up my phone trying to cop more work?"

Young Syke shook his head, quickly growing frustrated that Mob didn't see the possibilities in what he'd suggested. In his mind, he knew they were snakes. There was nothing anyone could say to change his opinion.

"I can see that you don't like what I'm saying," Mob spoke sincerely. "But you can't continue to think like that about people that we're in business with."

"Why not?"

"Because it's bad for business. Besides, I'm going to need you to start being the middle-man."

"The middle-man between who?"

"Guess."

"Come on, fam-o. You know I 'on't fuck with them niggaz like that. What happens when I have to blast one of them dudes for runnin' his mouth?"

Mob smirked. "I see you still caught up on some bullshit," he stated. "I'm trying to create an avenue so I can get back to handlin' my wax. You stressin' about some beef and them niggaz ain't even worried about you. Ain't you the one that suggested to let someone else take the wheel?"

Young Syke sat quiet for a moment, then reluctantly replied, "Yeah, but—"

"Ain't no buts!" Mob fired back. "I can't do this shit alone, while everybody sitting around doing nothing. You niggaz gon' have to step up to the plate and start handlin' some shit. The Crimson Mafia ain't what it used to be, either we gon' all come together and figure out how to make this thing work, or we can all sit back and watch it go down in flames."

"I wasn't sayin' I wouldn't step up to the plate," Syke explained. "I was just giving you something to think about. Do you really think it's a good idea for me to be their middle-man? I done bodied some of their homies and popped shots at the rest. Them niggaz probably hate the air I breath, and you can best believe they know I feel the same way about them."

Mob snipped out the rest of his blunt in the ashtray. Syke wasn't getting it. All the hatred he harbored toward the Steady Grinding Boyz wasn't doing nothing but slowing down business. "You wanna know what I think?" Mob asked snidely. "It sounds like you're trying to avoid them fools cause you afraid of something."

Young Syke looked at him sideways. "I ain't afraid of nothin'!" he replied.

"Well, stop trying to figure out a way out of this and do what tha fuck I'm telling you to. All that bullshit that happened back in the day, is dead! Let it go, fam. Focus on the money. Just focus on tha muthafuckin' paper, dawg."

Syke hopped up and walked over to peer out of the patio door. What Mob had just said struck a nerve, he wasn't afraid of nothing. The only reason he didn't want to deal with the Eastside, was because they were way too scandalous, and he couldn't trust them.

"Know that I fully understand everything you sayin' fam- o. All I'm trying to get you to see is— something ain't right about them niggaz. Maybe it's because we had beef with them, or it's something to do with Poncho. Needless to say, if you fuckin' with them— then I am, too! Just don't say I didn't warn you when shit goes South."

Mob was quickly growing tired of this debate. Young Syke was stuck in the past. All he saw was gang banging and revenge. The commas was what it was about now. Things had changed since Syke had been shot and left for dead. Business between the Crimson Mafia and the Steady Grinding Boyz was better than it ever was.

"Just keep in mind that we're trying to weather the storm," Mob reminded Syke trying to have empathy toward his feelings. "Ain't that how you put it? The only way we gon' be able to do that— is if you let the past be the past, is you with me?"

Young Syke nodded in agreement. There was no question whether he was down with Mob. He may have had a lot of unanswered questions, but Mob was right. Holding on to an old beef wouldn't do anything but slow business down.

"Say no more," he replied. "Whenever you want me to handle that shit—I'ma make it happen."

Mob sat silent for a moment as if he were in deep thought. "Tomorrow night, I want you with me when Lil' Menace comes through to drop that change off. That'll give you two the chance to meet and get an understanding."

Almost instantly anxiety had Young Syke stomach in knots. This whole situation had an eerie feel to it. It wasn't so much the idea of him meeting up with Lil' Menace, it was something else. Something that he wasn't quite able to figure out just yet.

"Do me a favor, fam-o," Young Syke began saying, "Watch them niggaz that we fuckin' with. I can't say what it is, but something tells me they're up to no good."

Smoke trailed from the tip of a cigarette filling the car with its toxic smoke. Everyone's faces inside the car were hard as stone, failing miserably to conceal the mischief they were dwelling on. Lil' Menace, sat peering through the passenger window of Big Crips money green convertible Glasshouse, the nickname for an early 70s model Chevy Caprice. He couldn't help but think about all the dope he'd lost when Freddy B had been robbed. Now instead of collecting the money to pay for a new package, he'd be forced to pay for everything out of his own pocket.

"So, how you wanna handle this?" Big Crip inquired. His face was contorted into a menacing scowl. No one in the car would look him in the eye. "That bitch April is gon' be calling expecting to pick that bread up soon. Plus, we still gotta meet up with Mob to drop that bread off. Everybody is gon' be lookin' to get paid around the same time. Is we good, or should we be preparing to mask up and put in some work?"

Lil' Menace hit the dipped cigarette allowing the smoke to trickle out his nostrils. He was numb to the dilemma he was facing. Taking losses was not part of the game that he could get used to. "We most definitely gon' have to mask up," he replied snidely. "Them bitch ass niggaz is stupid if they think that we gon' let them get away with this. I think it's time for them to feel our presence in the streets. Let 'em know that it's real consequences for those kinds of actions." Lil Menace passed the cigarette to Crazy Cuz who was in the back seat.

He'd remained silent, patiently waiting to hear what their next move would be. Either they could start another war with the Crimson Mafia or kill April and have one less person to worry about paying.

"What about the plan to find out where their stash spot is?" Crazy Cuz inquired. "Has that plan been thrown out the window? Because, if you plan on puttin' some heat on they ass, we can forget about robbin' them niggas. We'll never be as close to them again, as we are now."

Menace peered back over his shoulder. "Fuck robbin' them niggaz! I got my own money, my own dope, I don't need them fools for nothing."

Crazy Cuz glared at Menace. Lil Menace may have been the little homie, but he'd allowed himself to be blinded by the money he had.

"Chill out with that shit, cuz," Big Crip instructed them, spying Crazy Cuz through his rearview mirror. "Don't let this stuff get to you. We need to put our heads together and come up with a solution, not a means to create more problems."

Lil Menace looked at Big Crip sideways. It was easy to say, chill when he hadn't lost a dime. "I lost bandz because of the Crimson Mafia," Lil Menace spat. "When them bricks came up missin', I took that lick! I ain't tryin' to hear nothin' about being calm. All I wanna hear is that Draco spit when I'm hangin' out the window on they ass."

The tension inside the car was thick enough that you could feel it. Big Crip glared at Lil Menace with the devil in his eyes, and said, "Don't let that money fool you. Just because you down with tha hood, don't mean we won't get dead off in yo' ass."

Lil Menace smirked, yet, remained silent. There'd be no wins if he ever challenged Big Crip. The best thing he could possibly do was be cool.

"Fuck it!" he exclaimed. "If y'all niggaz so caught up in finding their stash spot, then that's what we gotta do. Let's just kidnap Mob tomorrow when we make the drop. By the time we get done beatin' his muthafuckin' ass, he gon' tell us where that stash is at."

Big Crip nodded and scooted lower in his seat. The plan Menace had just come up with, was the perfect idea to follow through with. Once they had the Crimson Mafia's stash spot, the streets would be theirs. There was no one left to stand in their way.

Chapter 8

Surprise Visit

The next morning, Derrick drove to work feeling a bit more cheerful than usual. The cool morning breeze that blew through the window was the announcement of yet another new season. Summer had long since passed leaving winter in its bloom. Electronic bells chimed as Derrick strolled through the doors of his women's clothing store. Mixed expressions of curiosity, recognition, and flirtatious stares lingered behind him as he hurried to his office in the back while glancing from left to right, he couldn't help but notice the many shoppers bustling amongst the aisles that morning, business had never been better.

Ever since Georgette had stepped up to become the new store Manager, business had been booming. The mix of her classy taste, mixed with his exquisite touch of sex appeal gave DF & Accessories a signature of its very own.

As Derrick neared the back of the store, he was caught off guard at the sound of someone calling his name, "Mr. Walker!"

He turned to see one of his employees rushing down the aisle headed in his direction. "I need to talk to you for a moment," Cynthia said. "I promise it won't take that long, but it's important."

Recognizing the anxious look etched on Cynthia's face, Derrick opened his office door and stepped to the side. "After you," he said. "Why don't you have a seat and give me a second to get things situated?"

Derrick moved about his office to get ready for the day. He'd arrived an hour and a half late to work, so he still had several important things yet to be done. Conversations with Cynthia had become part of the norm. She always had some bright idea about something that could help cause his store to function better. At times, Derrick wondered if Cynthia was a secret admirer of his. Besides the fact that she catered to his every expectation, her provocative style of dress seemed to be tailored just to his liking.

"You look nice today," Derrick complimented her as he poured himself a steamy hot cup of coffee. "Those pumps work well with the black bodysuit and skirt—" He paused and bobbed his head, then said, "Nice! If you don't mind me asking, where did you buy that outfit?"

Cynthia gave him a look laced with contempt and said, "I'd like to think that you'd recognize this outfit. Especially being that I bought it here."

"Really? I guess because I've handled so many different styles over the years, certain ones must've slipped my memory." Derrick sat down at his desk and carefully placed his cup of coffee on top of it. "I suppose I have to give credit to people like you for pushing us to supply such a unique selection?"

Cynthia smiled. "And that's part of the reason I came in here to talk to you."

Derrick leaned back in his chair and sipped his coffee. "Go on, I'm listening."

"I've been working here for over a year now. I helped Georgette come up with a marketing strategy that boosted our sales. And I've been hands-on in practically every other aspect of this company. The reason why I'm bringing all that up to say is—I'd like for you to consider moving me up to Management. You already know, I'm a hard worker, not to mention- I've helped train some of the other new employees. I have some new marketing strategies that'll make us competitive in the ever-growing online shopping area. And I truly believe I've got what it takes to help this company grow."

Derrick repositioned himself in his chair. feeling slightly uneasy about what he knew he had to say. Cynthia deserved the position that she'd asked for. Her work ethics were unparalleled. The only problem he had with moving her up, was the vow he'd made to himself. He could never allow someone that he could possibly be attracted to work close to him. After everything he'd gone through with April, he wouldn't dare risk being put in such a compromising situation again.

"Listen, there's a lot of truth in what you just said," he began. "I know how valuable you are to this company, and I appreciate hard-working people like you. But, contrary to what I see and believe, I only have need for one store Manager. Georgette has done a fine job with this store and don't think you, me, or anyone else can dispute that. So, although, I can't agree to give you the position that you wanted. How does a raise sound? I recognize what you've done for this company and I know your worth. A raise is the best I can do for you, right now. So, what do you say?" He'd hoped his decision would be met with signs of gratitude but judging by the awkward silence—it wasn't.

"Thank you," she replied half heartily. "Of course, I'll accept the raise. I could really use the extra money, and besides—you're right, Georgette does a fantastic job managing this store. I'd have some big shoes to fill had you chose to give me the position. But keep me in mind if you're ever in need of more management." Cynthia stood and quickly exited Derrick's office. As much as she wanted to continue to press for the position she needed, to do so might raise suspicion.

Business continued to go well throughout the remainder of the day. As the store hours finally drew near to closing, Derrick began pondering what he'd do for the evening. Relaxing at home sounded like the best thing to do, especially with everything that had been going on. But then again, he entertained the idea of going to the gym. He figured he'd pound out a few reps, maybe hit a couple of laps and call it night. It seemed like ever since he'd laid eyes on April, his lustful desires had built. All he needed was a release, and once he did, he'd be just fine.

Derrick threw on his black leather jacket and scooped up his brown leather satchel as well. His work at the store was done for the day. He'd decided to relax at home and get some much-needed rest. As he made his way through the store, he programmed the alarm before shutting off the lights. Everyone else had long since gone home for the evening, so he was the last one to leave for yet another night. After closing and locking up the store behind himself, Derrick caught sight of a Maserati creeping through the parking lot, headed his way. The extreme dark tint on the windows was a clear statement that someone wished to keep their identity concealed. But the fact that this person was creeping past his place of business said that this someone wanted their presence to be known.

Derrick slightly lifted his arms daring the car to stop. He welcomed whatever danger that came with such a bold move. The 9 mm that rested snug in the waistline of his Ferragamo trousers screamed for a moment to let loose. Luckily, whoever was driving the car must've felt it. They continued to pass on by never even tapping on the breaks.

"Is that someone that you know?" A man asked as he quickly approached Derrick from his left.

Derrick smirked and didn't take his eyes off of the car as it passed by. "As a matter of a fact it is," he replied sarcastically, already knowing who the man was walking up to him. "Is there something I can help you with?"

McCracken chuckled softly as he strolled up alongside Derrick. He casually slid his hands into his pockets and they both stood gazing out into the parking lot. "Mr. Walker, when are you going to understand that I'm not your enemy? I'm just a man that's trying to do his job. That's it. I'm not here to cause you any problems. My job is to make sure you're safe. And the only way I can successfully do that is— to lock up all the bad guys. Not you, the bad guys."

Derrick laughed forcefully. "Your job is to make sure I'm safe? What about my wife and son? Did you make sure they were safe? And let's not forget about my son's mother. You must've forgot to protect them. And what about—" He had to stop himself. He could feel his temper starting to flare. "Listen, do me a favor will ya? I don't ever wanna see you hanging around my store again. I've already told you once. I don t want your witness protection program. I don't need your help. All I want is for you to leave me the fuck alone! Can you do that?" Derrick glared at McCracken momentarily before turning to leave.

"And what if I don't want to?" McCracken yelled after him. "What if I wanna sit in this fucking parking lot until you finally start to see things my way?"

Derrick stopped just short of his car, turned back, and said, "Then you'll be hearing from my lawyer."

As bad as McCracken wanted to throw his weight around just to prove he was in control, he didn't. The FBI was building a case against one of the deadliest organizations the state of Oklahoma had ever seen, and Mr. Derrick Walker was a key witness.

***

Later That Evening

Derrick stood under the showerhead allowing the warm water to cascade over his body. The small encounter between him and McCracken was only more fuel to the fire that was already a full blaze. At times, Derrick didn't know if he was coming or going. He was too emotional, one minute he was happy, experiencing what he thought would be the best day of his life, and the next—he'd be ready to kill someone.

After finishing his shower, Derrick threw on some gym shorts and retired to the living room for his nightly meditation. This was the time he enjoyed the most, listening to music and allowing the melody to carry his mind to a faraway place. It was times like this when all barriers blocking his peace of mind came crumbling down. By relaxing and focusing on happy thoughts, he was able to escape to another place in time.

Derrick sat down in his usual comfy spot on the sofa and hit the power button on the remote. *Mic Lowry The Chase* streamed through the surround sound system throughout his living room. Instantly the smooth melody brought a smile to his solemn face, was he caught up in The Chase? Or was there a genuine attraction to the last few women he'd been with? Although Derrick felt he knew the truth to those questions. He'd like to believe he was genuinely attracted to those women he'd been with. The thought of being caught up in The Chase made him feel weak, vulnerable, and out of control. Easily misguided into the wrong path all behind the simple desires of the flesh.

The soft chime of his door-bell startled Derrick out of his light meditation. He was never one to have company. Only a handful of people actually knew where he lived. Derrick sat up on the sofa and turned the music down. He was just about to inquire as to who was outside. when he thought about the car that crept past his job earlier that day. Not only did whoever was behind the tint wish to keep their identity concealed, but they also wanted to make sure their presence was known.

Derrick rushed into his dining room and snatched up his gun off the dining room table. He checked the chamber to make sure it was ready to go and yelled, "Who is it?"

He listened intently for any noises that may sound out of place. When no one answered, that instantly heightened his sense of urgency. Derrick quietly shuffled down the hall toward the front door.

When he was close enough to peek out of the peephole he yelled again, "Who is it?" When recognition of the person standing outside his door registered, he snatched the door open.

"What in the hell are you doing here?" Derrick snarled, while partially concealing himself behind the door.

"I just wanted to make sure you were alright," April stammered. "I saw you at the club watching me."

"And!"

"An-an-an-and I just wanted to—" Suddenly April was speechless.

Derrick's hungry green eyes were enough to make the

most confident woman feel insecure. She felt naked, exposed, and guilty for having the nerve to show up at his door. But, regardless of how wrong she felt— she missed him.

"You just wanted what?" Derrick snarled, jolting April out of her stupor. "Just because you saw me at the club. doesn't give you the right to show up at my house!"

April peered down at the ground feeling embarrassed. After everything she'd put him through, what was she thinking? The last thing she ever wanted Derrick to think was that she was up to her old ways.

"I missed you," she solemnly stated. "I mean—I don't know what else there is to say. When I saw you the other night, all I could think about was us. What we had. What we could've had. What-what—"

"We didn't have shit!" Derrick snapped, glaring at her momentarily. "All we had turned out to be a nightmare. Whatever you think it was—it wasn't!"

"It might not have meant anything to you, but it meant the world to me and even though it hurts me to say this, I know I'm responsible for destroying it, I know that I am."

"Then why are you here?"

"I'm here because I'm sorry. I never meant for any of this to happen. I didn't want anything to happen to your family. I didn't want anything to happen to you. All I wanted was for us to be—" Her voice trailed away into silence as her emotions began to get the best of her. The burdens that Derrick carried she was being forced to carry them as well.

Derrick's menacing gaze slightly softened at April's openness. He stepped aside and opened the door as if to say she could enter. April timidly strolled past him unaware of his true intentions. She'd hoped because he had allowed her into his home that this was the first step toward healing their relationship.

"I want to thank you for being so understanding," she said as Derrick closed the door behind her. "I swear I never thought you'd—" Derrick was at her throat so fast she couldn't get any more words out.

He slammed her against the wall and placed his gun on the side of her head. "I lost everything because of you!" Derrick hissed. "My wife, my son, my friends—all dead!" He squeezed April's throat so hard that her face turned beet red.

She clawed at his hands, kicking and gasping for air. Derrick drug her along the wall until he'd reached his living room. Once April finally appeared as if she was about to give out, he shoved her down on the floor.

"Derrick, no!" she pleaded, coughing as she scrambled across the floor and crashed into the back of his sofa. "Don't do this. I-I-I swear I didn't mean for this to happen."

April's hands worked feverishly to get inside of her trench coat, but Derrick was already on her. He grabbed a fist full of her hair and slowly pulled her to her feet. Just as he put the barrel of his 9 mm back to her dome, the cold steel of April's .44 Bulldog touched the side of his neck, they both froze.

"Do you think I give a fuck about dying?" Derrick spat as foam peeked from the corners of his mouth like a venomous snake.

April didn't respond just yet. She simple stood peering up at him with the same penetrating gaze that he looked upon her with. If she hadn't had been so understanding to what fueled his anger, she'd have been pulled the trigger. Either they would agree to put down their guns and talk, or they both were going to die.

"I don't know what you care about anymore," April finally replied as Derrick pressed up against her, pushing her further over the back of the sofa. "But if you don't put that gun down—I won't be the only one that's going to die."

Derrick glared at her while plotting his next best move. He thought about trying to strangle her to death, but the next move would surely end in a showdown. He thought about all sorts of twisted fatalities that would ultimately end with April dead, but the smell of her sweet perfume had suddenly distracted him. This was the closest he'd been next to a woman since his wife had been killed. Something in the way April peered up at him, put him in the mind frame that she was his prey and he was the predator.

April nudged the barrel of her gun into the side of his throat, demanding a response. Just as she opened her mouth to give him his final warning, she felt the unmistakable rise of his manhood eager to meet her body.

She smirked. "This ain't what you want," she spoke softly referring to the guns that they held to each other's head. "But if you'll allow me, I'll show you exactly what you need." She cautiously leaned against Derrick forcing him to step back. Slowly she swiped his gun aside and placed her own on the back of the sofa. She gently kissed Derrick on the cheek while her hands roamed over his stomach, squeezing his chest finally pinching his nipple.

As their passion began to simmer, April slid her hand into Derrick's gym shorts. Finding the treasure that had led her to his doorstep she said, "Did you miss me?" She stroked him softly, massaging him pulling on his dick until it stood fully erect with no more than a menacing scowl from him. That was all she needed as confirmation to kneel and please him. April's tongue danced over the tip of his penis, licking and sucking it, before deep throating it. She could sense his ever-growing frustration for falling weak to her so she said, "Come with me."

April sauntered around the sofa and stopped in front of his ottoman. She unbuttoned her trench coat revealing a matching blue lace lingerie set beneath.

Derrick couldn't help but feel as if he'd fell in some sort of a trap. Had April known that a simple visit would lead to this?

As if reading his thoughts, April removed her coat and tossed it on the sofa. Her hands moved with precession removing her lingerie, panties and tossed them on the sofa as well. "Are you just going to stand there and watch? Or will you come over here and join me?" April laid back on the ottoman, propping up on one elbow. She hiked one foot up and gapped her legs open for Derrick to see. Her fingers appeared, then quickly disappeared, sliding in and out of her pussy. She tauntingly massaged her clit in circular motions just so he could see how fat and juicy her pussy was.

Derrick's monstrous green eyes roamed over April's body as he approached. Her once flawless skin was now covered in beautiful tattoo work. But the closer that he drew near, the more the horrific nightmare that they'd lived came back to haunt him. Hideous scars could be seen speckled along the side of April's body. The whens, the wheres, the hows, were all questions that needed answers.

April held out her hand, beckoning him to come closer and as he did she sat up. As soon as Derrick was within striking distance, he grabbed her by the wrist and snatched her to her feet. "Get all your things—and get the hell outta my house! And if I ever see you again—" he ran one hand up, along her neck and said, "I'll kill you."

Chapter 9

Undercover Work

In a secluded area on the outskirts of Oklahoma City. Agent Brown parked his white Durango on the edge of a desolate dirt road. His superiors had appointed places like this as designated meeting spots for debriefings. But with the weather quickly turning cold, Brown was becoming reluctant to continue to meet in those conditions.

"McCracken, Stevens," Brown greeted his superiors with a slight nod as he strolled up.

"Agent Brown, how's it going son? It's good to see you again." Stevens welcomed Brown with a firm handshake.

Brown went to stand between both men, leaning against their Suburban and peering aimlessly out into the wilderness.

"So, what's on the agenda this evening?" McCracken asked, getting straight down to business. "I'm sure those guys gotta be up to something."

Brown shrugged and shook his head. "Don't know," he replied. "For the most part, they keep me outta the loop of things. Usually, C-Loc wants to ride around making nickel and dime sells."

"Well, seeing as though that's how you met him," Stevens chimed in. "Maybe that's all Mr. Harris feels comfortable with exposing you to. After all, you did meet him at the carwash while getting your truck washed—" he suddenly paused as if he'd just thought of something. "—if I'm not mistaken, weren't you supposed to pick him up later this evening?"

"Yeah, but I still don't have a clue what they've got going on. One minute we're riding around doing a whole lotta' nothing, and the next we're trafficking drugs. Nothing is ever the same with this guy. Nothing."

McCracken scratched his chin, openly agitated by what he'd just heard. He hated to be in the dark about anything. He liked to know everything that was coming his way. "I can only hope that this is the chance that we've been waiting for," McCracken stated calmly. "If you're supposed to pick him up in the Parker Estates, who knows—maybe they've got intentions on bringing you further in on their operation?"

Brown thought about it for a moment, shrugged, and slapped his hands on his thighs. "Beats me, all I know is a time and a place. Everything else would be based on pure speculation."

McCracken peered over at Stevens and gave him the eye. He had great expectations for Brown, but his inability to give an affective debriefing troubled him.

"Is that what you're wearing to pick up C-Loc?" McCracken inquired.

Brown looked down at his Green Bay Packers hoodie and dusted off his jeans. "Yeah, but what does that have to do with anything?"

McCracken chuckled softly and replied, "*Everything!* If you want those guys to trust you, you've got to look the part."

Brown appeared puzzled. "And just how do you suppose that I do that?"

"For starters, I suggest that you carry yourself the same way they do. The Steady Grinding Boyz like to flaunt their money because they make tons of it. My guess is, if you present yourself as if you're already established in the dope game, they'll treat you as such. But if you come in projecting yourself like the average Joe Blow then they'll treat you accordingly."

Brown pondered his line of reason and said, "Correct me if I'm wrong. But you want me to simply act like I'm a high-level dealer, and you think that's going to get me in?"

McCracken shook his head. "Absolutely not! You've gotta talk like it, walk like it, and look like it. Those guys wear a bunch of jewelry. Jewelry is like saying, *Look at what I've got. I'm making a ton of money and you're not!*"

"But what if I don't have access to that kind of jewelry?"

"Then I'll just have to get you some. And what's with this crappy Green Bay Packers hoodie? You couldn't find anything better than that to wear?"

Brown held out his arms checking out his gear once again. "What's wrong with my hoodie? It's new."

"It looks cheap, I figured you'd make a better impression, than going over there in typical everyday attire."

"The Steady Grinding Boyz wear the Green Bay Packers gear because the G is for Grinding."

McCracken stood silent with a mischievous expression on his face. "Okay, I get it. I'll make sure you get some jewelry, and you make sure to do whatever you've got to do to get us into that organization."

***

"I wish I'd known that opening up a spot for tha family was going to be so much work," Young Syke said, sounding exhausted. "We've been in this bitch all day, and we still gotta pass out tha packs to tha homies."

Baby Jerk, a young lookout, spared a peek through the blinds. His job was to be on the lookout for any suspicious activity going on around their new spot. Now that Mob had given Syke the green light to open-up shop, there wasn't nothing up and coming rivals wouldn't do to get on top.

"As long as we do what we were told we're bound to come up!" Baby Jerk replied confidently. "We got the streets eatin' out of the palm of our hands again. In a minute—thangz will be back poppin' the way they are supposed to be." Baby Jerk took a swig of Hennessy and tried to pass the bottle to Syke.

"Nah, I'm cool on that shit, fam-o. We've been drankin' and smokin' all day. That shit gotta nigga feeling sluggish like I'm tired." Syke turned on the faucet in the kitchen sink and splashed his face with cold water. Suddenly, the room felt uncomfortably warm. He had to push his sleeves up on his thermal and brace himself against the kitchen counter. "It's hot in this bitch, fam- o."

Baby Jerk glanced back and noted the sickly look on his

face. "You a'ight, big homie? If you need me to I'll finish up the rest of the cooking. You just take my spot right here so you can rest."

Young Syke took a deep breath trying to shake off the strange feeling that had come over him. He picked up a dish rag and dabbed at his face, then he blacked out.

"Syke!"

Young Syke licked the blunt, then rolled it tightly. Ever since he'd returned from making a run, Bobo had been smoking like a freight train. The kitchen and dining room were blanketed with a light haze of crack smoke that was something Syke couldn't tolerate.

"Bobo!" Young Syke yelled. "When you gon' put that pipe down and do your job, fam-o? You gotta' get a grip on that shit, fam. I can't be up in this bitch smellin' crack all day." Reluctantly, Bobo put his pipe up and went outside. When Syke heard the backdoor slam he shouted, *"Finally!"* He was just about to spark up his blunt but quickly decided against it.

The house was layered in thick crack smoke. Syke strolled into the kitchen coughing and fanning at the smoke. *That nigga outta line for this shit,* he thought. *From now on that fool gotta go outside if he wanna get high.* When Syke opened the backdoor he stood face to face with a man with a gun.

"Syke!" Baby Jerk shook him repeatedly until he finally began to wake up. His eyes slowly opened but he was met by the aching pain in his shoulder.

"What happened?" He mumbled looking around the kitchen as if he had no memory of where he was at.

"You passed out, dawg. Now, come on so I can get you into the living room. You fell pretty hard. You need to kick back on the couch." Baby Jerk helped Syke up off the floor and guided him into the living room. Although he was small in stature that didn't stop him from doing anything.

Young Syke sighed heavily. "What the hell just happened?"

Baby Jerk helped him over to the sofa and they both sat

down.

"You passed the fuck out, bleed. One minute you was talkin' about how hot it was, and the next—*bam*! I ain't even get a chance to try and stop you. You just collapsed."

Young Syke shook his head trying to remember what had happened. He ran his hands over the back of his head, massaging another aching spot. "Shit was crazy fam-o. I dreamed about the night that I got shot. I was at the table rolling a blunt, and I told Bobo to do his job. The next thing I know—" Syke paused, at a loss for words as if something was bothering him. "When I opened up the back door, somebody was standing there."

"But why you go open the back door in the first place?"

"Because Bobo had the whole house smellin' like crack! Fam-o was goin' hard on that shit, and—"

"And what?"

Young Syke sat silent in deep thought for a moment, then replied, "All I can remember is his eyes dawg. Fam was shook. It was dark as shit. I think the nigga had braids. He looked like—" Syke took a deep breath while still trying to remember and said, "—man I don't know, it was too dark."

Baby Jerk nodded in understanding, then checked out the window. He didn't know the story that led to Young Syke being shot. Baby Jerk hadn't yet become a member of the Goon Squad. All he knew was that Young Syke had fainted, and whatever was the cause of it, was a problem that needed to be dealt with.

"Do you want me to call the homies?" Baby Jerk inquired.

Young Syke frowned and replied, "Call tha homies for what? We good over here. I know what just happened might seem crazy but let me explain. I was robbed over a year ago. And whatever happened to me that night I can't even remember. All I know is, tha homie Poncho found me slumped in a coma in Bobo's backyard. By the time I finally came to days had gone by. The doctor told me that my memory would come back, so I guess that's what's happening."

"That's some fucked up shit, dawg. So, I guess you passin' out is something that's about to be happening on the regular?"

"Hell—fuck—no!" Syke howled out in laughter. "That was the first time that shit happened."

"Well, whatever happened in the past, just forget about it. You scared tha shit outta me when you passed out. I can't have you dying on me up in this bitch."

***

Bang exited off the highway onto Kelly Avenue. He was nervous as shit. This was the closest anyone had been inside the Steady Grinding Boyz operation. Their click gave a whole new meaning to the saying, *Click Tight*. If you weren't down with the set, then you weren't allowed in their hood.

Bang's cell phone rang a special ring tone signaling that he had a call from C-Loc. He anxiously peered down at the screen while mentally preparing himself for what lied ahead. "C-Loc, what up?" He answered the phone. "I'm about ten minutes from where you told me to pick you up. Is everything still good?" Bang listened intently as C-Loc confirmed their meeting place. Yet, while C-Loc gave specifics on where to pull up and park at, Bang couldn't help but notice all the noise in the background.

"Damn, it sounds like y'all havin' a party over there?" Bang said. "Don't tell me y'all trying to kick it but didn't let a nigga know so I could be ready."

C-Loc wasn't the type to do too much talking over the phone. His main purpose for calling was to make sure Bang was still on his way. Opposed to answering any questions about who was there, or what was going on, C-Loc simply replied, "Just hurry up and get here!" Then hung up.

Bang turned on the street C-Loc had instructed him too, and immediately got a bad feeling. Kids paddled alongside his truck while anxiously trying to peer inside. The menacing scowls etched on people's faces as he drove by was a clear indication that he wasn't welcomed. Bang pulled to the curve in front of Big Crip's house as instructed. He carefully scanned the block noting several gang members watching his every move. It didn't take long before he decided to get out. He was just about to walk around his truck and head up to Big Crip's house when a little boy stepped to him.

"Who is you?" he asked.

Bang peered down at him slightly caught off guard and said, "I ain't cha daddy. I can tell you that much."

The little boy gave him a thorough once over and fired back, "Nigga, fuck you."

Bang burst into laughter. "Eazy there little fella'. Does your mother know you're out here talking to grownups like that?"

The little boy spied a curious peek over his shoulder then wiped his nose. "Who is you?"

Bang smiled. "My name is Bang."

The little boy looked as if he were trying to recall the name. *"Bang?"* he repeated. "You ain't from around here. What you doin' on my street?"

Bang eyed the little boy curiously because his aggressive approach was unsettling. He couldn't have been no more than 7 or 8 years old. He wore a pair of raggedy white sneakers with black Velcro straps. His hair had been neglected of a comb for at least a few days, and his face still bore the streaks from last night's drool.

"Whatchu' lookin' at?" the little boy asked.

Bang chuckled softly and replied, "Nothin', little man. I'm here to see C-Loc, is he around?"

Just then a woman that was several houses down stepped out on the porch and hollered, *"Treyvon!"* The little boy peered back with the fear of God in his eyes. "Get cho' muthafuckin' ass back over here in this yard!"

Treyvon nodded and quickly turned his bike around. Before heading back home he peered up at Bang and said, "You lucky my Momma wants me to go home. I was just gettin' ready to break you."

Bang laughed hard as the little boy took off peddling down the street. "This shit just keeps getting better and better," he said to himself, then adjusted his fitted cap and mobbed up to Big Crip's porch. "Is C-Loc here?" he asked a man that was sitting on the top step smoking a cigarette.

The man eyed Bang suspiciously and slowly rose to his feet. "Who tha' fuck is you, cuz?"

Once again, Bang was taken aback by someone else's aggressive demeanor. Had he not known any better, he would've easily mistaken the man as Lil' Menace. Despite the fact, that one had gold teeth and the other didn't, they both had the same facial features with their hair breaded to the back.

"My name is Bang, homie."

"*Homie?* Don't nobody know you around here, cuz. Just cause you here to see C-Loc don't make you my homie." The man opened the screen door and hollered for C-Loc, then quickly closed it back. Something about what Bang was wearing had caught his attention. He stood eyeing his clothing, openly showing his discomfort. "What's that supposed to mean, cause you got that on?"

Bang looked down at his hoodie that the man was pointing at and said, "I like the Green Bay Packers. I didn't wear it to make a statement or anything. I just wore it because I like the team."

The man slowly descended the porch steps while staring Bang in the eye. "Don't get this shit twisted, cuz. We don't do outsiders, and we damn sho' don't fuck with fake ass niggaz—" he paused and eyed Bang from head to toe. "Something about you reminds me of a fake ass nigga."

Bang gave a casual glance up and down the block. His special training was the only thing that kept him calm. He thought about going back out to the truck until C-Loc came out, but he didn't want to appear weak, so he took a deep breath and remained quiet.

"Leave that nigga alone, Crazy Cuz," C-Loc said as he stepped outside on the porch.

"I told cuz to come through, plus tha' homies tryin' to link up with him."

Crazy Cuz glared back at C-Loc, then grudgingly stepped aside. Had all of this not happened in front of Big Crip's home, Bang would've been tested.

"Don't worry about tha homies, cuz," C-Loc said as he led Bang into Big Crip's house. "Anybody is gon' get checked if you ain't officially a Grinder."

C-Loc had Bang wait in the living room while he went to do something in the back. The living room was furnished with old furniture, nothing lavish. The sofa and love seat still had thick clear plastic on it. The windows were covered by blue curtains which were the kind of curtains that they used back in the 80s. The floor was padded with cheap light blue carpet. Everything was outdated, from the floor model television to the big wooden coffee table in the middle of the floor.

Bang expected to see the notorious leader of the Steady Grinding Boyz soon as he entered the house, but instead, Lil Menace strolled into the living room and said, "What that Grinder life like, cuz?" Then went to take his seat on the love seat.

Bang was shook to his core. Everything he'd prepared himself to say had gone straight out the window. "Hey, how's it going?"

Menace was just about to take a sip from a bottle of Grey Goose but paused. "Who tha fuck says some shit like that?" Lil Menace got up and marched across the room. "You sound like tha' police, muthafucka. Loc, where tha' fuck you get this nigga at?"

Bang's mouth had suddenly gone dry. He nervously glanced from Lil Menace to C-Loc, while desperately trying to maintain his composure. "Hell nah, I ain't the police!" he exclaimed. "C-Loc will tell you, I'm all about my paper."

Lil Menace chuckled forcefully. "Oh, so you all about yo' paper?" Menace gave him a thorough once over checking out his chain and his gear. "Empty your pockets, playboy."

Bang peered over at C-Loc confused, but when he looked back at Lil Menace, he'd had his hand on his gun. Reluctantly, Bang emptied his pockets like he'd been instructed, and handed over his money as well.

"Let me get that chain off you too, playboy."

Bang peered over at C-Loc to see if this was some sort of a game, only to find him glaring back at him. "You should've known better than to come through here, flossin' in some shit like this." Lil Menace quickly slid his chain over his head and took a sip from his bottle. "You gotta earn the right to sport shit like this. Muthafuckas don't know you 'round here. You lucky you wasn't robbed and shot by a smoker or somethin'."

"I-I—just thought it'd be cool to wear this kind of stuff," Bang stammered. "I didn't know everyone was goin' be trippin' about it."

"You didn't know everyone was gon' be trippin'?" Lil Menace repeated, then peered over at C-Loc. "For tha last time—where tha' fuck you get this muthafucka at?"

C-Loc brushed past Bang and went to stand next to Lil Menace. "This the nigga I been telling y'all about. He the one that's been driving me around helpin' me get off all tha work. He also be coppin a lil' somethin', every now and again. But his money straight! I ain't never had not one problem. I think this is exactly the guy that we've been lookin' for to handle that one situation."

Lil Menace eyed him skeptically as he guzzled down some more of his drank.

Big Crip walked into the living room and tossed Lil Menace a bulletproof vest. "Put that on," he instructed him. "I already checked all the dough, we good on that. Now, all we need to do is figure out how we gon' get this nigga back to the spot. When and if we can manage to do that, then we can double back and deal with that bitch, April. This shit gotta go over smooth can't be no fakin'." Big Crip suddenly paused now realizing that someone else was in the room. "Who tha' fuck is this nigga?"

Lil Menace tucked his strap in the small of his back after putting on his vest. "This is one of C-Loc's people. Cuz just bought me this new chain as a late birthday present. C-Loc says he tha' perfect guy for tha' job, to get Mob back to tha' spot."

Bang looked from face to face trying to get a better read on what was going on. He had no idea what they were up to, but he could sense that something very serious was about to go down.

"You trying to get down with us?" Big Crip asked eyeing Bang curiously.

"Yeah. Why not? I mean, I've been doin' dirt with C-Loc. What else do I have to do?"

Big Crip smirked and said, "Is this some kind of a joke?" He walked over to the living room window and peered out into the front yard. Crazy Cuz sat on the top step watching out for the rollers and several Grinders could be seen on the block hustling as they always do. A white Durango sat parked in front of the house, but nothing looked out of place.

Big Crip peered back at Bang. Something about him made him feel uneasy, he couldn't say whether it was because Bang was an off-brand, a newcomer, or what the case may have been. All he knew for certain was that something smelled fishy. "Is that your truck outside?"

Bang glanced over towards the window. "Yeah, that's me."

"You got licenses and registration?"

Bang forced a weak laugh. "Everything is legit! My tags are up to date, blinkers work, and all that. Not to mention, my shit rides like a brand-new Benz."

Big Crip stepped closer so that he and Bang were face to face. "I need a driver," he stated seriously. "I need a muthafucka that's willin' to always be on point. A muthafucka that's down to move different things from point A to point B. Now, each load is subject to be different. Sometimes you're gonna have to be willin' to get your hands a little dirty, and sometimes you won't have to do nothin' but just drive. Seems to me C-Loc feels that you fit the build. But I'm askin' for myself. Can you handle all that?"

Bang swiped one hand over his forehead as his stomach began to churn. This was the opportunity he'd been waiting for. There was no question whether or not he'd do it. The only problem was he wasn't prepared. His truck wasn't equipped with any recording devices nor did he have any backup. Everything he did from that point on was off the radar.

Chapter 10

Tension Rising

The back of the Hill Side Courtz complex looked like a scene that was straight out of New Jack City. Smokers scurried around like zombies in search of their next hit, while Mob and Young Syke looked out at the courtyard from behind the dark tint on the windows of Mob's car.

"So, what did this nigga look like that you saw standing at Bobo's back door?" Mob asked while gazing out into the courtyard. He was having a hard time visualizing the dream that Young Syke had just told him about. Being that Syke could only remember part of the dream, Mob was left with several questions that needed answers.

"I can't explain it, fam-o," Young Syke admitted. "All I can remember was his eyes, dawg. He had this stupid look on his face. Like-like he was surprised that I even opened the back door." Suddenly Syke fell silent while struggling to make sense of what he could remember. He thought back to when he told Bobo to go outside, but that didn't help him remember nothing. He thought back to when he sat at the dining room table tolling a blunt but didn't help him either. After several confusing moments, Young Syke finally gave up.

"What's the matter?" Mob inquired, hoping to get Syke to say something.

"You mean to tell me that when you opened the back door, you just blanked out and can't remember what this muthafucka looked like?"

Young Syke sighed heavily. I know that shit sounds crazy, but—"

"Nah, that shit sounds stupid as fuck! How you gon' let some bullshit that happened over a year ago get to you? The nigga that robbed you is dead! I saw Poncho crush that fool in broad daylight. You need to stop stressin' over shit that's done and over with. All of this extra stuff you goin' through got me thinkin' that you looking for a way out."

"Never that, fam-o. I'm gon' always handle my business. It's just that stuff that I dreamed about felt real! I haven't ever experienced no shit like that." Young Syke turned to peer out the window. He'd hoped by them talking he'd somehow be able to remember what had happened. But, judging by the negative vibes he was getting from Mob, he simply decided to let it go.

"So, what do you think about our new spot?" Young Syke went on to ask changing the conversation to something more pleasing to Mob. "It's only been two days and we already got the spot jumpin' nonstop."

Mob nodded in agreement. The entire courtyard looked like a well-organized operation. Dealers worked inside their apartments while runners hustled around the courtyard making sales.

"You got this muthafucka looking the way that it's supposed to," Mob agreed. "You wasn't selfish considering the fact that you let the Hill Side niggaz handle the customers. That should give them a sense of security that you're not trying to muscle in on their turf. And even though we've been out here talking for over an hour, I still have yet to see any of the Goon Squad. That only means you must got them ducked off somewhere like they're supposed to be. That's the whole key to this shit. Outta sight outta mind."

Young Syke held out his fist to give Mob dap. "I'm glad to know that you're diggin' this shit, fam-o. I been going hard hoping to prove to you that I'm ready to move up in rank. I wanna be a boss in the Crimson Mafia, like you. I wanna be able to kick back and call shots or get a muthafucka's head blown off simply by making a phone call. The way I figured this out to be is, if you put Block Monsta in charge of the Goon Squad, and hired a few more cats, tha C.M. is gon' be stronger than it ever was. You can always bank on the fact that I'ma handle any mission to the best of my abilities."

Mob peered over at Syke and shook his head. "I see you're still not seeing the bigger picture. A title don't mean shit anymore. All this talk about becoming a Crimson Mafia boss, and leader of the Goon Squad—don't mean nothing. The only thing that matters out here is us! We the ones that's responsible for making sure things run smoothly. If we don't handle our bizness, then who gon' do it for us?" Mob scanned the parking lot and everything moving about. "Tell me, who do you think got these niggaz makin' this muthafucka pop the way it's been doing?"

Syke thought about it for a moment, but it didn't take long for him to come up with the answer to that question. He'd been hands-on in every aspect of running their new dope spot since they opened up shop.

"Me!" Young Syke exclaimed.

"And who're the only two people you know that's makin' sure the money is right and the pack keeps movin' from state to state?"

"Us!"

Mob nodded and gave Syke a moment to digest what he'd just told him. The whole time Syke had been worried about moving up to become a Crimson Mafia boss, he'd already been one. The illusions that wordplay played on him had him thinking he wasn't something that he already was.

"Leave all of that title bullshit for the working class," Mob stated seriously. "Out here, if you move like a lion and kill like a lion-then muthafucka yous a lion!" They both shared a brief laugh as Syke too nodded approvingly.

Now that he understood what position he held he vowed to emulate good leadership. "Not to switch the conversation so quickly," Young Syke spoke in between laughs. "But, what's the word on Lil' Menace? I thought we were supposed to hook up with his team today?"

"They're on their way," Mob assured him. "I just spoke with Menace over the phone before I pulled up. I told him to meet me here instead of at the body shop."

Instantly Young Syke's mind began to wonder. He wanted to make a good first impression. He wanted Lil' Menace to see that he was worthy of the position that he played.

"I should prolly' go get tha' homies ready?" Young Syke said opening the door to get out. "I want fam-o to know that it's not a game with me. If he ever gets outta' line than he knows what it's gon' be."

Mob chuckled and shook his head. "Well, you better hurry and get a move on it. I spoke with him over an hour ago. He should be here any minute."

***

"Turn up there where you see that car pulling out at," Lil Menace insisted as Bang drew near to the entrance of the Hill Side Courtz.

Once inside, Bang couldn't help but notice how well kept the property was. He saw young kids dart in between the apartment buildings, while they received an occasional head nod from a few elderly folks on their front porch. Bang hadn't seen anything that would lead him to think that something illegal was about to go down until they turned and drove deeper into the complex.

Gang members lined the sidewalk and parking lot. They were all dressed in red. Some wore red rags hanging out of their back pocket, others simply wore a lot of red. At one point, there wasn't so much as one piece of trash in sight, now the street was covered in it.

Bang made a mental note to drive normal because he didn't want to draw any unnecessary attention to them. He had a car full of gang members from another set. The wrong move could start a war. A war that he'd be trapped dead in the middle of.

"Cuz, said to pull around back," Lil Menace finally spoke, while peering anxiously through the window. "He said he'd be backed in along the fence in a burgundy Challenger." Menace pulled out his gun, checked it, then peered over at Bang. "Make sure to keep this bitch running no matter what! Big Crip, I need you to get out and carry the bag. Crazy Cuz, you just sit tight until it's time to do something crazy. We gotta make this shit look legit if we plan on making it up out of here."

Bang checked his rearview mirror watching as Big Crip and Crazy Cuz armed themselves. They were both strapped with semiautomatic weapons. Even if the police were to try and intervene they had enough firepower to hold them off.

"There his car go up ahead," Lil Menace said pointing toward a Burgundy Dodge Challenger, backed in along the fence. The windows on the car were dark tinted. It was hard to tell if someone was inside or not. "Drive past the car and park on the other side of him. If he ain't in the car, I'll hit him on his cell and let him know we out here."

Bang did as he was told and parked on the other side of Mob's car. He left enough space in between both vehicles just in case something went down. "If you plan on shooting at someone, don't you think it'll be a good idea if I turn the truck around?" he asked nervously, looking for any opportunity to stop whatever was about to go down. "We need to be in a position to get out of here fast! I'm sure as soon as whatever starts happening all of those people back there are gonna come gunnin' at us."

Everyone trained their sights on the people in the courtyard. There really was no need for alarm because most of the people outside were dope fiends.

"Peep game, cuz," Lil Menace snarled. "From now on, don't open yo mouth unless I tell you to. Your job is to drive, not think. Just drive. Leave all the figuring shit out up to us."

Bang nodded and peered back into the review mirror again. Big Crip was staring at him as if he suspected him of something, luckily, Lil Menace's phone rang.

"I'm out here parked by your car," Lil Menace spoke into his phone. "I'm in a white Durango. Hurry up, cause you already know how these niggaz be trippin' over here." Moments later Lil Menace ended the call and peered into the back seat. "Cuz was somewhere watching us the whole time. He supposed to be on his way, so y'all need to get ready. Them Hill Side niggaz is deep as fuck! This shit gotta go down fast."

Once again, everyone turned their attention back to the courtyard. Although there were several people moving about outside, they were still able to sift through the crowd and identify Mob and a small crew headed their direction. Three of the men appeared to be totting something heavy in their waists. Two of the men wore oversized coats too thick for the weather, and the last wore a black hoodie. Whatever he had in his waist was heavy enough that it gave him a hard time keeping his pants up.

"That's that muthafucka right there," Lil Menace spoke menacingly, breaking an uncomfortable moment of silence. "Cuz must've felt tha' heat. That's why he got all them hoe ass niggaz wit' him." Menace slammed his fist into the dashboard at the thought of his plan crumbling right before his eyes. They'd never had a better opportunity than they had now, and once Mob was out the picture, there was no one else that could stop them. "I say we stick with the plan and kill every last one of them muthafuckas. We didn't bring all this heat just for show. Let's let 'em have it!"

Big Crip watched as Mob marched across the courtyard and out into the parking lot. Not only were there no guarantees that they'd make it out of there alive, but they were caged in someone else's hood. No soon as the first shots rang out, the area would be crawling with Bloods. "We got too much to lose and not enough to gain," he spoke solemnly. "We brought the money as a back-up plan. I think it'd be best to pay this nigga and live to see another day."

"But what about April?"

"Fuck it—pay that bitch, too! Ain't no tellin' how many more people this nigga got watchin' us. If we hop out bustin', we might not make it back to tha' crib."

Lil Menace scoffed, hating the idea that he'd soon have to fork over all of that cash, but it was now or never. Mob was in the parking lot and almost to the back of the truck. "Come on, Crip, let's get out and pay this fool."

Mob walked up to the passenger side rear, as Lil Menace and Big Crip hopped out. From the looks etched on their faces, he could sense that something was wrong. "What up, fam?" he greeted them. "I'm surprised to see that you brought your peoples. Everything good?"

Lil Menace gave him a disapproving once over. "Yeah, everything is cool. I kinda figured you'd have these Goonies with you, so I asked tha' big homie to tag along."

Big Crip eyed Menace sternly. Now wasn't the time to get slick at the mouth.

"Here's the money that we owe you," Big Crip chimed in. "We had some other issues that had to get handled before we pulled up. I hope it's not a problem because I'm here?"

Mob glanced over at Menace, then peered down at the backpack filled with money. The idea to press the issue because of the open disrespect to the Goon Squad did cross his mind, but he quickly chalked it up as a possible mistake.

"I brought the *Goon Squad* with me so you'd have the chance to meet someone," Mob clarified. "From now on, this is who you'll need to deal with." Mob stepped to the side allowing Young Syke to come alongside him. "This is Young Syke. He's my right-hand man. Anything you need, you have to get it from him. When the time comes for you to drop off our money, this will be who you'll give it to. If there's anything you'd like to discuss with me, be sure and run it past him first. Are we clear?"

Lil Menace looked upon Young Syke like a man would a judge after being sentenced to life in prison. *How can this nigga still be alive?* he thought. *I shot that fool at point-blank range ain't no way he should be alive!*

"Damn, fam-o. Either this nigga don't know what to do when a person is trying to introduce themselves, or he must be star struck."

Menace's eyes fluttered when he realized how he must've

looked. But gun or no gun, he'd never allow a Crimson Mafia member to try and stunt on him. "Cuz, you got tha' locsta fucked up!" he spat. "You think I give a fuck if you was a star or not?"

Young Syke reached for his strap, threatening to pull it. "You gettin' smart, fam-o? I can easily show you what I do to a nigga that think they wanna test me."

Big Crip quickly realizing that the situation had gone from bad to worse stepped in and shouted, "*Syke!* We ain't come here for all this, youngsta. I already tol' y'all that we had some other shit going on before we got here. Don't trip off the small shit, let's stick to talkin' about the money." Big Crip looked to Mob hoping to get some kind of assistance but received just the opposite.

"You came to our place of business, disrespected my niggaz, and never once did you stop and think about what was gon' happen?" Mob glared at Big Crip in disdain. If Lil Menace was bold enough to step to them with disrespect, then he was bold enough to deal with the consequences.

"This shit ain't gotta go down like this, gangsta," Big Crip said. "We had an agreement. The streets is finally eatin' again. The hood is straight. We still holdin' true to tha' truce."

"Nigga, fuck a truce!" Young Syke barked. "We can take it back to the way this shit is supposed to be if you want to."

Big Crip ice grilled him, wishing they were in a position to give him exactly what he was looking for. But being that they'd already put their guns up, the best thing they could do was walk away.

"All your money is right there in the bag, youngin;," Big Crip spoke sternly and dropped it on the ground. "Business been good ever since the truce started, so if you don't mind— I'd like to keep it that way." Big Crip gave Lil Menace the nod to get back in the truck. "Whenever y'all ready for us to pick up the next pack, get at me. I guarantee nothin' like this will ever happen again."

Big Crip got in on the passenger side back seat, while Lil

Menace got in the front. But as they backed out of the parking spot, Lil Menace and Young Syke locked eyes. "I shoulda' blew his fuckin' head off," Syke snarled. "I heard that slick comment when he called us some fuckin' Goonies." They all burst into laughter while Mob stood calmly watching as the Steady Grinding Boyz left.

"Block Monsta, Baby Jerk," Mob said. "Y'all two fall back to the spot while I holla at Syke." As everyone strolled across the parking lot leaving them alone, Mob turned to Young Syke and said, "Tha' fuck part of the game is fakin' like you gon' pop something?"

Young Syke's head snapped back. *"Fakin?"*

"You heard me, *fakin*'! You did all that barkin' and ain't shot shit. The only thing you accomplished by doing all that dumb ass shit was showin' them niggaz what kinda strap you got."

Young Syke sighed forcefully. "I ain't buss because I didn't wanna fuck business up. We just got the spot started. I didn't want to do anything unless you gave me the word to."

Mob laughed forcefully. "Tha' fuck I need to give you the word for? Being a boss means you should know what you can afford to lose and what you can't. You gotta know when to let that steel bark, and when to let a nigga live. Besides that, ain't you in charge of tha Goon Squad? Your job is killin' muthafuckas ain't it? Why should I ever have to tell you to do your job?" Mob started walking and left Syke to figure things out on his own. Mob had bigger fish to fry. Whatever other lessons Young Syke needed to learn, it was time for him to learn them on his own.

***

A warm fire burned bright, casting shadows across a beautifully polished wooden floor. The luxurious amenities that adorn the dimly lit study danced to life as flames lapped at the roof of an extravagantly built fireplace.

A man of Mexican descent sat in a tall leather wing back chair. His gaze into the flames seemed distant, dreamy, almost unaware of anything else going on around him. Without taking his sights from the flickering flame, he reached and took a small glass of Irish Whiskey from the table next to his chair. The liquid fire was his favorite remedy to heel his throbbing headache. In all his years of being the boss of a boss, he'd never allowed his feelings toward a woman to come between his better judgment, until now.

Plocko was a man of infinite power throughout the Midwest and deep into the dirty south. His connections with Drug Lords in his native country were solid, unbreakable. Bonded by blood, Plocko was placed in a position of power in the United States. His job as a boss consisted of creating a pyramid effect. This tactic allowed smaller crews and organizations to get money under the watchful eye of the Cartel. Plocko taught these crews structure, giving them names, titles, and roles that everyone played all to obtain ultimate control.

In the wake of Plocko's success, he encountered a courageously cunning go-getter named, Slim. Slim was the epitome of what a true boss was. His thirst for money and power was unmatched. In a game where players were misled to believe that quantity of dope meant they controlled the game, Plocko taught Slim the real definition of power. If you rule by inflicting terror, the game will forever be yours.

Slim's rise to power was bittersweet. He killed anyone who dared stand in his path and became the supplier of everyone that didn't. Slim rightfully donned the title of Under Boss of Plocko's empire. Everyone Plocko supplied was now supplied by the Crimson Mafia. By passing control of distribution to Slim that enabled Plocko to disappear off the scene. He became like a ghost in the streets, yet his power could still be felt.

In time, Slim held the streets and everything in them in the palm of his hand. The cars, the houses, the jewels, were all just luxuries he'd loosely indulged in. But when a beautiful woman by the name of April Jordan came into his life, Slim's whole world was turned upside down. He laced April in nothing but the finest. Anything she wanted, he made sure she had it. Anything she needed, she had it without ever having to say a word. Slim went so far as to teach his Queen to be everything he'd been taught and even went so far as to in introduce her to Plocko. In the event that something bad ever happened to him, he wanted April to be capable of maintaining his organization.

Upon the very first moment that Plocko laid eyes on April, she became an object of his desire. Although he'd never been one to lust over a woman, something about her drove him wild. But being that April already belonged to someone else, Plocko applied patience. Being a middle-aged man, he'd gained great success due to discipline. He knew that in time he'd get exactly what he wanted and in time—he did.

Plocko groaned at the thought of the terrible predicament that he'd placed himself in. The thought to hurl his glass of whiskey into the fireplace surfaced in his mind, but he quickly dismissed the idea. Nothing that he'd been informed about was proven fact. The rumors circulating throughout the underworld had no merit. Outside of April's suspicious movements, nothing that he'd heard or saw led him to believe that she was a snitch.

Plocko's thoughts were interrupted when the door to his study began to creak as it opened. Bright light from the hallway poured into his dimly lit study. The soft clicking sounds of high heels crossing the hardwood floor alerted him of April's presence. Due to his uncertainty about the rumors, Plocko remained calm revealing nothing about what he'd heard.

"How long are you going to sit in here drinking in the dark?" April asked.

Plocko's eyes roamed over her provocative style of dress and Fishnet revealing perky nipples. Her hand rested defiantly on her hip. "You've been in here for well over three hours and you haven't said a word to me. Are you going to stay mad at me forever about last night?"

April's all-night disappearances had already been established as unacceptable. For her to come into his study using seduction as a means to cover her trail only heightened Plocko's suspicions.

"Oh, so you're still not going to say nothing to me," she went on as she kneeled before him. She crawled up to his legs and uncross them, then began nibbling at his inner thigh. "I already told you I was with my friends. What else do I have to do to prove to you that I'm not lying?"

Plocko peered down at her for the first time. He hated anyone trying to play on his intelligence. But instead of allowing her to think that she could outwit him, Plocko kept his emotions in check. "I don't know?" He finally admitted using a husky Mexican accent. "You say you were with your friends, I say okay. You tell me you do nothing." He shrugged. "I say okay. What more do you want me to do?" Plocko sat his glass back on top of the table. In a weak attempt to stand, he leaned forward hoping April would move.

"I'm not done with you by far!" April snapped, then gently bit his bottom lip, and kissed him. "I have a surprise for you being that you've got so much on your mind. I brought home some entertainment that should easily do away with your frustrations."

Moments later, a beautiful dark-skinned woman emerged from the hallway walking slowly into view. She wore nothing but a black robe that was conveniently opened exposing her neatly trimmed pussy.

Plocko chuckled. "This for me?" he asked, smiling as the woman removed her robe and carelessly tossed it on the floor.

"No, my love," April replied summoning the woman closer with just the wave of her finger. "This bitch is for us!"

The woman came to tower above April who still sat comfortably on her knees. April tapped the armrest, commanding the woman to place her foot on top of it. She then spread her feminine folds and buried her face in the woman's crotch. Her tongue danced over the woman's clit causing her to moan. Plocko couldn't help but assume this wasn't the first time that they'd done this. The way the woman took hold of April's head, rolling it around, fucking it. She made it perfectly clear they'd been together before.

As if reading his thoughts, the woman looked upon Plocko with lustful hunger in her eyes. Her beautiful long hair partially covered her face as she bit into her bottom lip. "Come fuck me," she whispered. Almost instantly, Plocko began to unbutton his shirt, when he stood to remove the rest of his clothing, the woman took hold of his hand and placed it on her breasts. "They feel good, don't they?"

Plocko was speechless. These weren't the type of games he was accustomed to playing. The woman that he'd fell madly in love with was a beast, a master manipulator, a goddess in her own right. While one woman caressed his chest, fingers roaming through his peppered hair, the other unbuckled his trousers. Before he knew it, he stood naked before both women.

"I want you to fuck this bitch just like she told you to," April spoke seductively. "All your anger, frustration, and negative energy, let it go inside of her." April sat down in his chair and cast her leg over the armrest.

Using the simple pat of her hand against her crotch, the woman got down doggy style. She slowly crawled up between April's legs nibbling at her fishnet with her teeth.

Plocko kneeled behind her, palming her ass cheeks, rubbing his thick slab of meat between them. He wanted to fuck that bitch so bad that he already began to smear pre-cum down the crack of her ass. Just as he began to have second thoughts, the woman took hold of his dick and guided it inside of her.

"Unnnhhhh," she moaned as he slid deeper. Her pussy was amazingly wet, her fingers were instantly covered in her own juices.

When Plocko saw how turned on she was, he couldn't help

but wanna pound away. *Clap! Clap! Clap! Clap! Clap!*

The woman bucked and squirmed while throwing her ass back at him. *Clap! Clap! Clap! Clap!*

"That's right!" April exclaimed. "Fuck that bitch,"

Plocko clawed at her ass cheeks pushing them together and spreading them apart. He drove as deep as his manhood would allow him inside of her, then gasped. Cum decorated her pussy lips like snow on the lawn of a perfect Christmas morning.

April grabbed ahold of the woman's head and forced it back down between her legs. The devilish smirk across her face was a silent celebration of what she'd managed to accomplish. Plocko wasn't the type of man to meet new people. He never allowed people outside of his closest comrades anywhere near him The fact that she was able to pull this off was easily one of her greatest accomplishments. She knew Plocko would be furious about her not coming home last night, so she made a few arrangements. Arrangements that the average man would fall for.

April smiled triumphantly as she watched Plocko pound away on one of her hoes. Not only would her transgression be overlooked, but now she could easily return to Texas unnoticed and check-in.

Chapter 11

Back To The Old Me

Derrick sat staring in a daze at his computer monitor. All he could think about was April. The way she touched him, her looks, her body, the scars. As much as he hated to admit it, April had awakened something inside him. His desire to be with a woman was at an all-time high. From the moment April walked out of the house he'd been at odds with himself.

Derrick groaned and rubbed his weary eyes. To say he was exhausted would be, to say the least. He'd been up all night contemplating his next move. Should he go back to the club and find out more about, SGB? Or should he take his chances and find out what McCracken might be able to tell him?

Strangely enough, no matter what idea he'd managed to conjure up his thoughts always wandered back to April. She was the missing link, the piece of the puzzle that brought everything together. It was because of her that this nightmare had begun and it'd be because of her that this nightmare would soon come to an end.

Two gentle knocks at his office door stirred Derrick from his thoughts. He quickly scooped up a stack of papers rearranging them, trying to appear busy. "Come in!"

Cynthia greeted him with her beautiful smile and said, "Good morning. I hope I'm not interrupting anything?"

Derrick lifted his hands up. "If you were, then mission complete. Now, what is it that I can help you with?"

Cynthia slowly walked into his office, her eyes wandering all over the room before finally landing on him. "I was wondering—Fitted 4 A Don is going to be open tonight. I was hoping you'd come have a drink with me. This won't be like a date just more along the lines of having fun."

Derrick appeared to *give* it some thought but quickly dismissed the idea. "I've got tons of things that need to get taken care of. The winter—"

"Please? It'll be fun. All I see you do is work. It'll be good for you to switch things up for a bit."

Derrick laughed and replied, "I enjoy what I do. For me, it's all about preparation and staying focused. Get it? Maybe that's something you need to focus on."

Cynthia's eyes narrowed. "Oh, I've always been focused," she replied snidely. "I'm so focused that I make sure and take care of everything you're not focused on."

"Oh, yeah, like what?"

"Your office. Every morning when you get here, I already have a pot of coffee waiting for you."

"And?"

"I make sure you eat when things get so hectic around here that you miss lunch."

"Annnnddd?"

"Annndddd—I work extra hours and never once have I asked for a dime. Now, if that isn't being focused, I don't know what focused is. Get it?"

Derrick laughed hard. "Okay-okay-okay!" He exclaimed. "I'll go to the damn club and have a drink with you."

"Really?" she inquired, excitedly.

"Why not? Outside of working myself to death, I really don't have any plans for the evening."

Cynthia clasped her hands together and brought them to her chest. "Good! Since you don't have no other plans for the evening. What time will you be picking me up?"

Derrick's eyes bulged. "Damn, just like that? I'm the designated driver?"

"You've seen my car. It's little, but if you don't feel comfortable driving, I'll come pick you up."

Derrick thought about that for a moment. "Nah, don't worry about it," he conceded. "It'll probably be best if I drive anyway. How about I pick you up   around seven?"

"Seven sounds great!" Cynthia replied and made a hasty retreat out of his office. Although Derrick had his assumptions about how Cynthia actually felt about him, he understood that having fun was just part of who she was.

Cynthia was the happy type, always curious, giggly, but often very outspoken. She was a very attractive woman that could've easily had her way with most men. But, despite her beautiful looks, Derrick only regarded her as a good friend. She'd become the only person he could talk to. Besides her openness and being willing to voice her opinion, Derrick could count on her to keep it real. If ever he'd done something that he shouldn't have, she wasn't afraid to tell him.

A soft sigh escaped his lips at the thought of the possible mistake that night could be. This whole nightmare started the moment he began letting his guard down and having fun. That's why he was so relentless about staying focused. Although that night may have been a harmless night out on the town, temptation would always loom in the shadows.

***

6:45 P.M.

Derrick pulled up outside of Cynthia's apartment and parked. The soft glow seeping through her blinds gave her home a warm inviting look. Derrick got out just as a strong gust blew snatching up his collar, forcing him to stumble backward. He quickly tucked his chin and charged into the stiff wind. When he reached Cynthia's door, he hoped she'd be on the lookout expecting his arrival. But judging by the amount of time it took her to answer the door, she wasn't.

Cynthia must've had a million and one locks to unlock just to let him in. All he could hear as the click- click-scrap-click-scrap sounds of several locks being unlocked. But soon as her front door finally came open, he could see why she was so heavily protected.

"Hello-hellooo," she greeted him in a sing-song manner. "Welcome to my humble abode. I'm sorry if you had to wait outside for too long."

"Yeah, I bet," Derrick joked. "I told you I'd be here around seven."

Cynthia giggled softly as she closed and locked the door behind him. "You know how most men are. One minute you'll be somewhere by seven and the next you're three hours late!"

Derrick smirked. "But I ain't most men. My business thrives because I stay in tune with the time. And besides, I thought you'd be dressed and ready by now."

Cynthia rolled her eyes playfully and replied, "Just give me a few more minutes. I have to change this skirt because it's got some kind of a stain on it."

Derrick looked around Cynthia's apartment surprised by how neat, yet modest it was. Pictures decorated her walls and end table, some of which he had to wonder if the people in them was friends, or family. None of the people looked anything like Cynthia. In fact, several of the pictures still had the paper pictures of models used for advertisement. To most, that might seem rather odd, but then again— that could have been because of any number of reasons.

As Derrick continued to roam around her living room, checking out the pictures, flowers, and decor, he yelled out, "Almost ready yet?" He peered down at the only photograph he'd found thus far.

"I am," she replied, leaning against the wall behind him. "Do you like what you see?"

Derrick spun around, slightly startled by her sudden presence. "Oh, the picture?" He looked down at the picture, then back up at Cynthia. The picture, then back up at Cynthia. The picture—then back up at Cynthia. "Oh, yeah-yeah-yeah. What is this like—a glamour shot or something?"

Cynthia giggled and sauntered over to the dining room table to get her purse. "I guess you can call it that if you want too. The car dealership took it when I purchased my first new car."

Derrick coughed, fumbling with the picture as he returned it back to its place on the mantelpiece.

"What about you, are you ready?"

"Oh, yeah-yeah-yeah, sure," he replied. "I've been ready. I was just looking around your apartment for a bit until you got ready." Derrick hurried over to the front door but stopped just short when he noticed that Cynthia hadn't budged. "Something wrong? You're still coming, right?"

Cynthia sucked her teeth and nodded her head. "You look nice," she said sarcastically.

Derrick looked down at his clothing trying to figure out what she was hinting at. His Jimmy Choo oxfords did look exceptionally stunty. His Black Burberry coat, trousers, and shirt all looked on point. He tugged at his long-sleeve button-down shirt, pulling it over his gold Rolex watch. He brushed over his diamond earrings, straightened his Ray-Ban glasses, and adjusted his coat. "I do look mighty fine if I may say so myself," he replied arrogantly.

"Pleassseee," Cynthia growled, glaring at him through tiny slights. She slung her purse over her shoulder and walked over to the front door. "What are you waiting for?"

Derrick opened the front door slightly taken aback. "Did I miss something?"

"Hummmm, I don't know. Did you?"

Derrick chuckled. "I really don't know that's why I'm asking."

"Oh, yeah-yeah-yeah," she mocked him. "How about, you like nice Cynthia. Or, you have a nice home, Cynthia. Or how about—"

"Damn! My bad."

Cynthia held up one hand silencing him and said, "Save it. Most men would've known to compliment a woman's taste. But like you said—you're not most men."

Forty-five minutes later, they walked through the doors of Fitted 4 A Don. The bar was jam-packed, buzzing with laughter and music. People of several ethnic backgrounds could be seen engaged in idle conversation. Some casting curious looks in their direction, others huddled up simply talking.

Derrick scanned the room as they wind through the crowd. Luckily, he was able to spot a table in the back and led the way over to it. He was starting to feel as if he'd overdressed for the occasion. Most of the people there either wore jeans, sweat suits, or something equally as comfortable.

"Do you think I'm a little overdressed for a bar?" he asked and stopped in front of the table where they'd be seated.

"Why would you think that?"

"Well, look around. I thought this was supposed to be some kind of a club, not some hole in the wall bar?"

Cynthia frowned, Fitted 4 A Don might not have been a club, but it sure as hell wasn't some hole in the wall bar, either. "It's not about what you have on. It's about coming out to this place and simply relaxing. This about being you. Look around—people are dressed in all kinds of stuff." She sat her purse on the table and removed her coat as well. "Would you say that I'm overdressed as well?" She slowly twirled around showing off her black leather minidress. The top was a mixture of leather and lace complimenting what Derrick had on.

"You look amazing," he said, then removed his coat and placed it on the back of his chair. "But you did not buy that outfit from me!"

Cynthia laughed. "If I did, it's not like you would've remembered anyway."

Derrick dismissed her comment with the swat of his hand. "Yeah, but I'd remember this," he assured her and flagged over a waitress. "I'm ready for a drink, how about you?"

Cynthia dug into her purse and fished out a few dollars. "That's fine. But I'm going over there to put on some different music." She pointed to a small jukebox across the room by the window.

"What would you like? Something strong? Fruity? A Daiquiri maybe?"

"I'll have a double shot of Tequila and a Long Island." She winked, assuming the type of liquor that she'd ordered would catch him off guard. Most men that she'd dated weren't accustomed to having a female drinking buddy, that could go round for round with them. As Derrick would soon find out, Cynthia wasn't your average female.

Hours and several drinks later, *Miguel's Going to Hell* bumped through the bar's speakers. The crowd raved with excitement as Derrick and Cynthia prepared to embark on a challenge that would end with only one winner. How they'd ended up in that competition was unknown to either of them. They were drunk, having fun, and neither of them could see beyond claiming victory.

Derrick stared wild-eyed at Cynthia over the rim of his mug. Malt liquor trickled from the corners of his mouth as he guzzled down his drink as fast as he could. There was no way he'd allow Cynthia to beat him. Not Cynthia, no way never!

Cynthia stared back at Derrick with the same mock expression, but not so much as one drip escaped her lips. Had Derrick known better he'd have known that he was no match for her.

"Done!" she exclaimed and slammed her goblet down on the counter. The crowd erupted into cheers while Derrick stood gasping for air. *"Ha!"* She celebrated in his face. "I'll bet you didn't see that coming." *Hiccup!*

Derrick shook his head in disgust, refusing to stand there and listen to her taunt him. "Yeah-yeah, who cares?" he uttered and began to make his way back through the crowd. "It's obvious that my glass was much bigger than yours was. That's the only reason why you won."

Cynthia's mischievous giggling could be heard behind him as they made their way back to their table. But, with each step, Derrick could feel the buzz from the liquor getting stronger. "I'm hella' faded," he spoke over his shoulder. "What do you say if we call it a night before we end up stuck on the side of the road somewhere?" Derrick looked back expectantly, only to find that Cynthia was standing in the middle of the aisle laughing to herself. *Hiccup!* She was clearly just as faded as he was. His next question was answered without her having to say a word.

Derrick drove Cynthia straight home. He'd hoped that the cold night air would take some of their buzz away, but by the time they arrived at her apartment, the cold air had proved to do just the opposite.

Hiccup! "Oh, Derrick," Cynthia slurred. "I had such a great time tonight. Didn't you?"

He scoffed, he couldn't afford to entertain her foolish gibberish. It was freezing cold, there was a million and one keys on her keyring, a million locks, she was drunk, and she kept sliding down the wall. "Damn it, Cynthia! Which one of these fucking keys goes into these locks?"

She slowly lifted her head off the wall and slurred, "What, that keeeyyyy?" She pointed at the light fixture above their head.

"Cynthia!" Derrick shouted, frustrated by their freezing predicament. In a last attempt to try and unlock the door, Derrick stuck another key into the keyhole and *bingo*, it worked.

The warm air inside Cynthia's apartment instantly washed over him sending chills down his spine. Derrick led Cynthia over to the sofa and helped her get comfortable. "You've been a bad girl tonight," he said teasing her because she was drunk. "I'm going to need you to stay right here and get some rest. I'll call you in the morning."

Cynthia giggled. "Derrrrick, I'm sooo sorry for being a baaaddd girl tonight. I promise it won't happen again."

Derrick chuckled. Cynthia looked so cute lying there in her drunken state of a complete mess. Her long curly hair laid partially covering her face. Her feet dangled over the edge of the sofa rubbing together, in a vain attempt to kick off her Tom Ford boots. She reminded him of Paula Patton, because of the way her face shown in the dimly lit room. Derrick kneeled next to her and helped remove her boots. Just as he was about to get up, he noticed the strange expression etched on her face.

She was about to blow.

"Hold it!" Derrick's eyes darted from one corner of the room to the next in search of a trash can, finding none— he ran into the kitchen and snatched up one out of the pantry. Just as he rushed back into the living room and slid the trashcan in front of her face, she threw up.

Errrrrghhhh! Nothing but stinky alcohol poured into the trashcan.

Errrrrrrghhhh! Now it was stinky alcohol and something that looked a lot like chicken. Derrick's heart went out to Cynthia. After all the liquor they'd consumed, he was surprised she'd lasted that long. He sat on the edge of the sofa patting Cynthia's back to calm her down. But just as she finally began to relax, he caught a whiff of the contents inside of the trashcan.

He gagged. "Wait-wait, hold on for a second," he mumbled reaching for the trashcan. He took a deep breath because something didn't feel right, then he gagged again. "Let me—" he tried to swallow it, he tried to think about something else, but then it happened, he threw up.

Errrrrghh! Nothing but stinky alcohol splashed into the trashcan.

Cynthia giggled.

Errrrrrghhhh! Now it was stinky alcohol and something that looked like a piece of hamburger.

***

Mob sat behind dark tint while he scoped out a small Mexican bar. His target was known to be a regular at the small establishment, but there was no telling when he'd come out. Mob had to keep a close eye on his truck, the front door, and everything else moving about outside. If he missed this opportunity, he'd have to wait for another time to do this all over again.

A few hours had passed since Mob felt the warmth from

the car heater. Out of fear of giving away his position, he waited in the freezing cold. The front windshield of the car was covered in fog so bad that he occasionally had to wipe it off with his sleeve. Everything had changed now that it was time to put in work. But this was also part of the game that he so dearly loved.

The thrill of the hunt, the excitement of baiting the trap. The sudden splash of blood he saw when a bullet exited the dome of one of his victims. Mob growled softly, unable to control his ever-growing anxiety. His thirst for bloodshed was so intense that he unconsciously sat squeezing the handle of his gun.

The door to the bar swung open as the target's driver stumbled over to a champagne-colored Ford F-350 truck. Mob toyed with the idea of hopping out and crushing him right there in front of the bar. But, what about the target? What about the several other Mexicans that came out behind him? Mob had several angles that he had to consider while he waited to see what would happen.

To his surprise, none of the people that came out with the driver were with him. Each of them went their separate ways as the driver hit the alarm on the truck and climbed inside. White steam poured from the exhaust at the rear of the truck. Mob could only assume that the driver was warming up the truck for the target. Mob zipped up his tan jumpsuit and pulled his skully down snug over his forehead. He opened the door and quickly made his way across the parking lot.

Just as he neared the back of the Ford F-350, the driver hopped out and ran to the back of the building. Mob stopped dead in his tracks, positioning himself against the truck. To keep from looking suspicious, he walked up to the driver's side back door and climbed inside.

The truck's interior consisted of soft leather seats and a partially smoked cigarette burned in a portable ashtray. Mob peered over to the passenger's side front and rear. The front seat was empty. No weapons in sight. The rear had a white plastic bag on the floor filled with small boxes of car parts. A pair of red and black jumper cables sat directly next to them. The driver would no doubt return at any moment.

Mob had to think fast. He pulled out his gun ready to kill the driver upon his return but quickly decided against it. The sound of gunfire might alert people inside the club that something bad was going on. He had to be creative if he expected to pull this thing off.

The driver emerged from behind the building trotting at a slow pace. His head was down so that his cowboy hat shielded his face from the blistering winds. His fingers worked feverishly at his belt buckle as he made his way back to the truck. Surprisingly, he stopped and peered up at his truck curiously. His gut must've warned him that something was terribly wrong, but nothing looked out of the ordinary. His truck still sat idling just the way he'd left it. The interior of the truck was as black as the night, concealed by dark limo tint. The headlights cast bright light up against the building.

"I must be tripping," he uttered softly to himself and climbed inside.

Mob slung the jumper cables over the seat knocking off his hat as the cables were wrapped around his neck. The driver fought for dear life, but Mob had already gained the perfect position on him. He dug his knees into the back of the seat, pulling with all his might. The leather seats crackled. The driver's feet fluttered. The engine roared to life. His neck snapped.

Pop!

The adrenaline rush that Mob felt was indescribable. His eyes bounced around the truck's interior as if he were high off-speed. Moments later, the target emerged from the bar with two beautiful women under his arms. They all stumbled toward the truck but ended up with the target pinned against the wall. One woman groped his crouch while the other guided his hand over her ample breasts. He squeezed them, then quickly broke free from the two women waving goodbye.

The target scurried over to the passenger side of the truck and got in. But before he had a chance to notice that his friend was dead, Mob had his steel pointed at the back of his head.

"If you move—you're a dead man."

The target slightly peered back over his shoulder and said, "Do you know who I am, guy? You're pissing on tha wrong tree, ese. If you leave now, I might just let you and your family live."

Mob laughed forcefully. "I oughta' put a hole in the back of your head for even saying some stupid ass shit like that."

The target slowly shook his head in disappointment. "What tha' fuck do you want, ese? You lookin' for money? Dope? Women? I no have none of that shit! You can take whatever cash I have left in my wallet and get the fuck outta my truck."

"How about you give me some information to help me solve a puzzle?"

"Tha fuck do you think this is, ese? This ain't Jeopardy, and I damn sure ain't no snitch! You think I'm scared of you because you got a gun pointed at my head? I no scared of you, vato. You scared of me! That's why you've got the gun."

Mob smirked he knew this crazy muthafucka believed every word head said. "I want you to listen and listen closely, Juan—" He paused and leaned closer, then went on to say, "That is your name isn't it?" The target started to reply but stopped and nodded. "Now, I didn't come here to kill you. I came here to find out some very important information. But if you choose to try and play these stupid ass tuff guy games—" Mob pulled the hammer back on his gun and let the silence speak for itself.

"Alright-alright, guy. What is it that you want to know?"

"I want to know the truth about what's been going on."

Juan scoffed. "You think just because you know my name that entitles me to tell you something? There are a lot of things going on."

"Like what?"

"Like you ruined my night to get some pussy. My friend Fernando here is dead. And you fucking ruined my got damn truck that cost—"

Boom!

The blast from Mob's gun nearly busted the man's eardrum. "Don't play with me, Juan. I know a lot more than you think I do. I know you're position in Plockos organization. I also know that you oversee his operations. Now you can try and play a game with me if you want to but I assure you—I'm not here to play with you."

Juan sat silent for a moment massaging his ear trying to stop the ringing. He wanted nothing more than to kill whoever was in the back seat, but he was slightly puzzled as to who it could be. Not many people knew him by his real name. The only way someone would know him by Juan was if they'd dealt with their organization before.

"Mob?" Juan inquired.

"Now why did you have to go and guess my name?" Juan tried to turn around but Mob buried the barrel of his gun in his cheek. "Not so fast, damu. The first shot was just a warning. The next time I pull this trigger—you'll be the highlight story of the Daily Oklahoma."

Juan sighed forcefully already knowing that he was dealing with a savage. "What did I do to you, guy? This city is yours because of me. We treat you like family."

Mob snatched his head back and positioned himself next to his ear. "How tha fuck do you treat us like family? We pay for everything that we get from you muthafuckas. The city is ours because we put tha work in for it to be. Don't sit here and try to tell me shit about family. Y'all steady feeding us with a long-handled spoon."

Juan peered into Mob's eyes for the first time. Although he'd saw him on numerous occasions, never once had he been on the wrong end of his gun. "Alright, amigo. Let's just take it easy for a second. I'm not in the business of selling information, it's not my job. All I do is what Plocko tells me to do."

Whap!

Mob smacked him with the butt of his gun. "Who said anything about buying some information? You're gonna tell me everything I wanna know and be thankful for every moment I let you breathe. Now, what do you know about this new dope that's been flooding the streets that's stamped with, T.O?"

Juan dabbed at the blood trickling down his face and replied, "What make you think that I know anything about, T.O?"

Whap!

"Because if you don't—you'll wish that you had. Plocko isn't about to allow just any muthafuckas selling dope unless he's got his hands in it somehow."

Juan sighed and forced a soft chuckle. "I told the boss that this was not a good idea, but he is in love with the girl. He give her everything, guy. Money, cars, clothes, her own stamp. You name it, she's got it."

"Hold tha' fuck on. What do you mean, her own stamp?"

"T.O.," Juan stated with emphasis. "T.O. means Take Over. That is the stamp she wanted on all her bricks. Plocko gave her the green light to hustle here in the city. I'm sorry, my friend, but I no have nothing to do with it."

Mob's mind was reeling. The Crimson Mafia had been nothing but loyal to Plocko. Why the Cartel would want to cross them out, was blowing his mind. "Who is this bitch?" Mob snarled. "Since Plocko is allowin' some punk ass bitch to hustle on our turf, I wanna know who she is and where can I find her."

Juan groaned. Not only had what he'd just revealed put his life in danger but what he was about to say would surely start a war. "April," he replied solemnly. "Slim's ex-girlfriend is the one that is behind Take Over. She lives with Plocko in the country, but it'll be impossible for you to—"

Boom!

100

Juan's blood splattered across the windshield as he fell dead. Only death could right the wrong of betrayal. If Plocko had chosen to do business with a lying, conniving snake over the Crimson Mafia, then he too had chosen death over life.

Adrian Dulan

Chapter 12

New Friends

The next morning came bearing warm sunlight raining down into Cynthia's living room. The sound of bacon frying mixed with the Lifetime melody coming from the television awoke Derrick from his sleep. His stomach rumbled, demanding immediate attention, but as he sat up nausea threatened to overcome him once again.

"What happened to me last night," he moaned while cradling his throbbing head. "I must've passed out drunk while we were talking."

Cynthia peeked out from the kitchen and asked, "Are you all right in there?" She walked into the living room carrying a tall glass of cold water. "Here drink this. There's a bottle of Aspirin over there on the end table."

Derrick gratefully excepted the glass of water as she turned and hurried back into the kitchen. After reaching over to get the pill bottle, he removed a couple of tablets and quickly washed them down. "What time is it?" he asked looking around on the floor for his cell phone.

"It's just after twelve."

"Twelve? Shit!" Derrick flung the covers back and immediately reached for his shoes. "I have to get home and get dressed for work. Georgette is probably swamped over at the store."

Cynthia giggled softly while she sauntered back into the living room with a tray of breakfast. "Relax," she insisted. "I already spoke with Georgette earlier. Everything is fine at the store. She said they've got everything under control. She told me to tell you to focus on feeling better." Cynthia set the tray of food next to Derrick and removed a plate for herself.

"You told her that I had a hangover?" Derrick asked in utter disbelief.

Cynthia shrugged. "What else was I supposed to tell her?

If I'm not able to go in because you're asleep on my living room floor. Don't you think I should tell her something?"

Derrick laid back on his pillow now staring up into the ceiling. Cynthia had a point. "I guess you're right. I just don't want anyone jumping to any conclusions, because we had a friendly night out on the town." Derrick rolled over and propped up on his elbow. "So, how long have you been up?"

"I've been up since the crack of dawn. My mental alarm clock won't let me sleep even if I got a little tipsy the night before."

"A little tipsy, you say?"

Cynthia squinted her eyes. "A little. I brought you a pillow and blanket, but I guess you were too drunk to budge. I literally had to lift that big ol' head of yours just to get the pillow under it. But when I spread that blanket over you it was a wrap! You snuggled in and instantly started snoring."

"*Did* I?"

"Did you."

"I must've been hella tired not to mention we had a full day at work. I can't remember the last time I mixed malt liquor with shots of Tequila. My stomach is churning at the thought of what I did to myself last night."

"But did you have a good time?"

"Without a question. It's been a long time since I've had that much fun. And seeing as though you were the one that came up with the idea, I am forever grateful."

Cynthia blushed. "I thought surely you'd say that you were never going out with me again. After the way things turned out with you getting drunk and all."

"That's all part of it. Quite frankly, I never get out to do ordinary things like that anymore. I'm always consumed with—" he had to stop himself. He suddenly realized that he was saying way too much. The best thing for him to do at this point was change the conversation before he said the wrong thing.

"You're always consumed with trying to run your store,"

Cynthia said assuming she'd completed his sentence.

"Yeah, the store," he lied and took a few bites of his food. "So, what's your story? Do you go out much? What do you do in your free time besides get on my nerves asking a million questions?"

"Get on your nerves?" she replied snidely.

"I'm just kidding. I said that cause I knew I'd get a reaction out of you."

Cynthia held her fork up and twisted it at him. "Don't make me use this on you," she growled. "And no, I don't go out much. I usually go workout after work, come home, cook, clean, and get ready for the next day."

"That sounds a lot like my daily routine. I normally go to the gym after work, go home, and basically do the same thing as you." Derrick sat up and leaned his back against the sofa. The more he sat talking to her, the more he became aware of how much they had in common. "What about family and friends?" He went on to say. "I'm sure you've got someone that you like to hang out with?"

Cynthia sat her plate aside seemingly thinking of the proper response. "My family is back home in Ohio. I don't have any friends. I guess that's why I'm always getting on your nerves!"

Derrick laughed. "Yeah right. There's not a woman in the world that doesn't have any friends. Women like to do too much talking not to have any friends."

"Have you stopped to think that's why I'm always talking to you?"

"Well—no. I mean—I've thought about it."

Cynthia laughed. "I'm very cautious about who I spend my time with. I don't wanna look up and find myself in a shit load of trouble because of somebody else's mess."

Derrick couldn't help but look off and start staring at the television. Her last comment had hit too close to home.

"So, what about you?" she went on to ask. "I never hear you talking about your personal life. You don't have any pictures of family members around the office. And you never talk about anything outside of DF & Accessories."

Derrick grimaced, he had to tread lightly when it came time to talk to people about certain things. But truthfully, he clearly remembered Cynthia having met his wife before. True, he hadn't worn his wedding band since she was killed but how could Cynthia have forgotten?

"I'd say that we're the same kind of people," Derrick finally replied. "My folks stay way in another state, and as far as hanging out— I'm a full-grown man now. Times have changed. Hell, people have changed. Things are nothing like they used to be."

"I can agree with that. But what would you say if I told you that I had another idea?"

Derrick shook his head. "I'd tell you I'm not going out to the club until I recuperate. Look at me, I'm still dressed in yesterday's clothes because I passed out drunk on your floor."

Cynthia laughed. "Going out to the club again wasn't my idea," she assured him. "I was thinking more along the lines of us becoming partners."

"What, like business partners?"

"No silly. Workout partners!"

Derrick looked at her like she'd lost her mind. "Yeah, right, I really don't think you'll be able to keep up with me."

"Why should I have to keep up when I could be doing my own thing?"

"Well, I thought you wanted to be partners?"

"Partners in that we're there to encourage each other to stay on track and keep going. At the end of the night, we can hit a few laps and line out a few details for the following day."

Derrick had to think about that for a moment. She was offering something that he really needed. He needed someone to keep him grounded, focused, and someone to keep him from losing touch with reality. The only thing he feared was the emotional attachment that could come with that. Too many lives were at stake and the last thing he wanted was to bring someone into this nightmare.

"Listen, before we go any further," he began saying. "Let's get a few things understood. I don't mind having a workout partner, just as long as you're serious. When I exercise I go hard. When I work I go hard. When I do anything—"

"You go hard. I get it. Going hard is what's to be expected. But let's not forget who was the one that went hard and won last night."

Derrick burst into laughter and said, "This isn't about drinking up the damn bar. This is about exercising, remember?"

"I know. I know. But I still stand by what I just said."

"And that's why I'm willing to give this thing a chance. Partners?" Derrick held out his fist for a fist bump.

"Partners."

***

April laid in bed gazing up into the blue skies speckled with tall white clouds. Her thoughts of her toxic reunion with Derrick was at the center of her attention. The way he tasted, his chest, the look in his eyes when he came to the point of almost killing her, were all things that had her panties moist. But lustful thoughts weren't the only things April had in mind. Derrick was one of only a few men she'd been with that could offer her the lifestyle she'd always wanted to have.

Being that the streets was a cold, unrelenting place to try and make a living, everything she'd worked so hard to achieve had been violently ripped away from her. Because of Slim and his savage pack of goons, she'd been banished to live in secrecy. Having the threat of death always on her heels and the FBI monitoring her every move, it was going to take a miracle to get back to the place in life where she once was.

Thoughts of Derrick slowly began to settle back into her mind. He was the owner of the perfect venture for someone in her shoes to want to be part of. If she could somehow work her

way back into his grace, maybe she could become a silent
investor. Maybe even expand his store, or better yet—help
open several new locations. Those ideas alone were enough to
bring a smile to her solemn face. But after the way he'd acted
the other night, getting back into his grace might prove to be a
challenge in itself.

April sat up and quickly grabbed her purse from the foot
of the bed. She hurriedly searched for her cell phone and
immediately dialed Derrick's number once she'd found it.

"Hello," Derrick said answering his phone on the first ring.

"Hey, it's me," April replied.

Derrick had to look at his phone again, only to find that it
was an anonymous caller. "Who's me?" he asked.

"It's April. Are you busy?"

Derrick sighed heavily into the phone unable to believe
that she had the nerve to be calling. "What in the hell is wrong
with you? Didn't I tell you to stay the fuck away from me, and
that I never wanna hear from you again?"

The line was quiet for a while before April finally
responded, "I just wanted to talk, Derrick. That's all, just talk."

"Talk about what, April. I already told you once we ain't
got shit else to talk about."

"But we do! Don't you think we need to talk about what
happened? What about last night. What about us? What about
our future?"

"*Our future?* Do you realize how stupid you sound, right
now? You should be thankful you still have a fucking future. I
should've done away with your ass last night."

"What if I told you I could give you something? Something
I know you'd want?"

"I swear this shit just keeps getting better and better.
You're just rambling off the first thing that comes to mind,
aren't you? The world doesn't revolve around sex, April. You
can't get what you want just by offering sex to someone."

"Who said anything about sex?" she replied snidely. "I can
give you the people that killed your family. I know all Slim's

associates from A-Z. The only problem is—I don't have your attention."

Derrick was speechless, his thoughts bouncing from the night he'd saw her at the club, to SGB, to the Crimson Mafia. "How do I know you're not just saying this just so that I'll talk to you?"

"Because it's not all just about you, Derrick. I want those muthafuckas dead just as bad as you do. I might not have lost people I love like you have, but I almost lost my life. Had it not been for the Feds raiding when they did—then I'd be dead."

Once again, Derrick's mind was reeling. Although he wished death upon April he wanted nothing more than revenge for the death of his loved ones.

"If I told you, yes, we could talk somewhere. Where would you want to meet? I've got Federal Agents staked out in front of my store, and there is no telling who's following me."

"I've got a quiet place down on the beach," April replied. "I'll fly you out to Miami and neither of us will have to worry about being followed."

Derrick laughed. "Sounds like a setup if you were to ask me. What kind of sense does that make for us to fly way out to Miami so we can talk?"

"There's too many eyes and ears in Oklahoma. I wish I could just bring you out to where I am now, but that probably isn't a good idea either. Just look at it like a vacation."

"*A vacation?* This sounds like you're up to your ol' bullshit ways again?"

"That's a two-way street, Derrick. And for the record, it's not whatever you think it is. I just figured it'll be safer if we get as far away from the city as possible. You don't understand how deep this thing goes. I can't tell you over the phone, but I can say that it's bigger than you ever imagined."

"So, I'm just supposed to abandon discretion and walk into the unknown so we can talk?"

"That might sound crazy, but yes."

"Who's supposed to pay for all of this? You're talking about vacationing and all of this crap. Am I supposed to be your sponsor?"

"I haven't asked you for a dime. I don't need your money, Derrick. You'll have a plane ticket waiting for you at the airport. You don't have to worry about clothes, food, or anything. All you have to do is be there."

Derrick toyed with the idea for a moment, but there was no doubt in his mind what his decision would be. As long as he kept his guard up and a cautious eye out for danger, he figured everything would be all right.

***

8:00 PM

McCracken pulled up outside of Stevens' home and parked on the street. It had been another long day filled with countless dead ends and frivolous twists and turns. The weight of the case had long since begun to take its toll on both Agents. But now that their leads had ran cold, both Agents were looking for a way to close the case.

"What does the D.A say we need to have in order to shut this thing down?" Stevens asked unbuckling his seat belt.

"He says we need to figure out who the woman is that's been contacting Lil' Menace," McCracken stated as a matter-of-factly. "Regardless, that she keeps switching phones we still have to find a way to locate her."

Stevens leaned on the armrest, tapping his index finger on his temple. Whoever the woman was, she was sharp as a tac. She knew to change phone lines at least once a month. Not only did she change lines, but she also went out and bought a brand new phone each time Agents came across her voice on wiretaps, surprisingly, she'd suddenly change numbers. The fact that she had so many numbers made it difficult for the FBI to track her.

Stevens turned to see that his wife was standing there glaring at him.

"I think we need to bring Mr. Johnson in on the conspiracy," Stevens said. "You know as well as I do, once we start throwing around potential prison sentences people tend to talk."

McCracken smirked. "Sure, they do, but will he? Once we bring Lil Menace in, if he doesn't talk, it's over. Whoever that person is we've been listening to on those wiretaps will disappear. We need whoever that person is, and everyone connected to them."

"Yeah, you're probably right. Dinner is probably ready, and she hates it when I let my food get cold." They both shared a brief laugh as Stevens told his wife he'd be in, in a second. "One more thing before I go," he continued. "I think it's about time for us to bring in Agent Davis on some of these debriefings. We need to have everyone on the same page, that way they know what we expect of them."

McCracken sat peering out of the driver's side window. His mind had been so cluttered with cracking the case, he couldn't sleep at night. Often, he'd be up into the wee hours of the morning rummaging through old paperwork and listening to wiretaps. This case had become an obsession.

It's time to do something drastic, he thought. *If that means serving a few indictments, so be it.*

"You know how much I hate rushing," he went on to say. "But I'm starting to feel like we're losing control of this thing."

Stevens nodded in agreement. But, as bad as he wanted to close the case, he didn't want to miss one vital link. "Agent Brown's next debriefing is tomorrow morning," he said. "Let's hope he made contact with Lil Menace. That will mean we're on the right track."

"You just don't know how badly I want that to be true," replied McCracken.

"I think I do. But if Brown doesn't have anything helpful, we'll start serving indictments. Then, we'll find out if those guys really can stand on a code of no snitching when they're faced with life in prison."

That brought a smile to McCracken's face. "Sounds like an early Christmas present. I can't wait to put an end to all of this madness," he said, as out the corner of his eye he saw Steven's wife step out onto the porch and stand there with her hands on both hips. "I think Margaret is about to kick your ass if you don't high-tail it inside," he joked.

"I think you're right. I'll see you in the morning." Stevens climbed out of the car.

Chapter 13

The Brink Of War

Plocko awoke at the crack of dawn anxiously awaiting the arrival of his men. News of Juan's murder had sent the Cartel into an uproar. Plocko vowed to avenge his fallen comrade. For someone to kill one of his trusted Lieutenants was no less than a cry for war.

Plocko descended his steps with a look of determination etched on his face, wearing nothing more than black silk pajamas, black slippers, and a black robe that bore his initials, he strolled into his study preparing to lay down the law. However, he saw fit to deal with Juan's death would without question stand. Nothing or no one would dare try and trump his orders.

A beautiful young maidservant scurried in behind Plocko quickly removing the curtains that covered his massive windows. She hastily tied them with a cord then went to tend to Plocko. Plocko watched her every move like a hawk. He drummed his fingertips on top of his desk while loosening a Cuban cigar with his other hand. To anyone else, his gaze might seem intimidating, or downright menacing. But to her, it was a look she knew all too well.

"Will there be anything else you need me to do, senor?" the question she'd asked was rhetorical. The lustful hunger in her eyes was but to reciprocate the vibes she felt coming from Plocko.

Plocko grunted softly allowing a mischievous grin to form on his face. He leaned over placing his cigar to his lips and she lit it. Plocko took long hard puffs at his cigar while peering up into her eyes. Her beauty was mesmerizing. His thoughts instantly gave way to their x-rated moments. His dick slapping against her chin as his cum spewed across her face. Nutt dripped from her lips to her breasts, where she eagerly lapped at it with her tongue, massaging it into her skin.

"When my guests leave, I want you to come back and see me, okay?"

The young woman appeared to give his orders some thought but later would not do. Just as she was about to reply, a knock at the Plocko's study door, silenced her.

"I see you had no problem finding my home," Plocko spoke to several of his men as they strolled into his study. "Come in, have a sit. There is much that we have to discuss." Three men went to sit on a leather sofa along the wall. Two went and stood guard by the massive fireplace. Luis, who was the new second in command, took his seat right in front of Plocko's desk. "Maria, bring all our guests something to drink. I imagine that they're thirsty."

He gave her a stern look that said they'd continue where they left off, later.

"Gentlemen, someone very dear to me has been taken," Plocko puffed at his cigar and intentionally blew the smoke across his desk into Luis's face. "Tell me why."

Luis nervously shifted in his chair. He leaned forward and placed his elbows on his knees, then quickly sat back trying to appear at ease. "I don't know, senor. We have been studying the footage from the tapes night and day, but there is nothing."

Plocko chuckled and stood up. "You know nothing?" he said. "Are you sure that is the story you want me to believe?" Plocko ambled around his desk, studying Luis with mock interest.

"Senor, we looked at the video and saw nothing! I tried to—"

"Silence!" Plocko shouted. "I'll hear none of that. When I ask you why my friend was taken from me, you'd best to give me a reason why! So, I ask you again. Why was my good friend taken from me?"

Luis glanced back at his men over by the fireplace. Both of them had their faces twisted into menacing scowls. "They-they-they want what you have," he stammered.

Plocko smiled and squeezed his cheeks. "Good answer.

They want what I have." Plocko slowly began to walk around his study looking at the many paintings that decorated his walls. "I want you to comb every inch of this city until you find the person that's responsible for doing this. And when you do—cut his fucking head off." Plocko stood gazing up at the head of a young buck that he'd mounted to the wall. "Yes," he laughed. "Cut his fucking head off!"

A gentle knock at Plocko's study door drew everyone's attention toward it. "Sorry to interrupt," Maria said. "Here are your drinks." Maria hurried into the room carrying a small try of cups of coffee. But with Plocko being on a seek and destroy mission, everyone declined her offer, except for one.

"Gracious," one of Plocko's men said with a smile, accepting the cup of coffee that Maria had offered him.

"Senor," Maria spoke in a hushed tone and quickly made her way over to Plocko. "I have to go and buy groceries this morning. Is there something special that you'd like for this evening?"

"Hmmph," Plocko grunted. His attention was drawn to the assassin that sat gingerly sipping at his cup of coffee. "He wants what I have, no?"

Maria looked clearly confused. She had no idea as to what he was talking about. "I'm sorry, senor. I don't understand."

Plocko paid her response no mind. He strolled around the room and over to the man that sat gingerly sipping his cup of coffee. *Sips!* "Let me see your gun," Plocko ordered and without hesitation, he jumped to his feet and handed Plocko his weapon.

Sips!

"Look at this guy," Plocko spoke mockingly. "He gave me his gun." Plocko looked around the room bobbing his head. He cocked the gun and peered down at the man. "Do you want what I have?"

Sips!

The man chuckled softly and replied, "No-no, senor. I'd never want such a thing." He took another sip from his cup, but

the menacing scowl etched on   Plocko's face had finally
registered to him. "I'm sorry, senor. I-I-thought it was okay to
drink. I no want nothing that you have."

Plocko waved the gun back and forth in his face. "Oh, no-
no-no. You drink up. The coffee is good, no?" The man peered
down at the cup in his hand and reluctantly nodded. Plocko
peered over at Maria and pointed at her. "You want some of
her pussy?" The man was visibly shaken and quickly shook his
head. Plocko placed the barrel of his gun next to the man's
nose. "You sure you no want some? She mine. It is very good,
yes."

To lie would surely warrant death, but to admit his lust-
fueled secrets would too. Plocko lowered the gun and said, "I'll
let you think about that for now. But the next time I ask you
about her, you tell me, okay?" Plocko strolled back around to
his chair and sat down. But, before he continued with his
meeting, he sent Maria on her way.

"There are a few more things I'd wish to discuss today.
One being, I want to know why April has to make these
unexpected visits back to Texas. I want to know where she's
staying while she's away, and who she's with. If it is a man—
" he paused and sliced his hand through the air. "Chop his dick
off. I want it brought back to me in a box. I'll have Maria serve
it to April over a candlelight dinner. I also wish to know if she's
working with the FBI. There has been some very disturbing
news that has reached my ears. I must find out if any of it is
true."

Plocko turned his attention to Luis and looked him dead in
the eye. "I want you to contact Slim's attorney and find out
what he knows. If it is a cheap lawyer, fire him! I want nothing
but the best representation for the man that has remained loyal
through these trying times." Plocko placed his gun on top of
the desk. He took his time puffing at his cigar before
continuing. "I want everyone in this room to understand
something. No one, and I mean no one—takes anything from
me. Not even the Feds!"

***

Mob walked out of Daylight Breakfast with several bags of food for the Goon Squad. Several days had passed since the last time he'd spoken to Young Syke. Now that he knew Plocko had a hand in flooding the streets with more dope it was time to bring his team up to speed. Mob hit the alarm on his rental car unlocking the doors. He quickly slid inside and piled all the bags on the passenger's seat. Soon as he'd started the car and put it in reverse, a white Durango came to a screeching stop narrowly missing him.

Mob glared through the review mirror, before reluctantly slamming the car in drive to allow the SUV to pass. Surprisingly, the white SUV pulled in the parking spot right next to him. It took everything inside Mob not to hop out and act a fool. But if the police got involved this minor infraction would surely turn into much more trouble than it was worth.

The passenger door of the Durango opened and a beautiful woman slid out. She smiled and waved before heading towards the restaurant. Mob couldn't help but watch her hips sway as she sashayed toward the front doors. The way her ass rolled in her black skirt had his undivided attention. But as he continued to sit there watching, the driver of the Durango came into view. For some odd reason Mob suddenly felt uneasy. He knew the man but couldn't remember from where.

Mob strained, peering through the review mirror to get a better look. But the further that they walked away, the harder it was to see them. Just as he began to back out, he noticed two white men appear out of nowhere. It was obvious that they all must've known each other. The driver walked right up to them and shook hands with them.

As Mob went on to observe, he noted three big bold letters on the back of the men's jacket, *DEA*.

"Damn!" he snarled and went on to pull out of his parking spot. Just as he drew near to the exit preparing to turn out into traffic, it hit him. He did know the driver. He'd been in a shootout with him the day that Poncho was killed.

Mob thought back to when the man jumped up from between the cars and yelled, *"Freeze!"*

His head was spinning. He'd like to think what he'd just saw was all in his head, but it wasn't. He remembered how adamant Young Syke was about how things weren't adding up. If the Feds weren't involved back when Poncho killed that man, they most definitely were involved now.

"What it do, fam-o?" Young Syke greeted Mob upon him walking into the spot. "Seem like months done gone by since the last time that I saw you."

Mob chuckled softly and handed Young Syke the bags of food. "I told you I was about to get back to handling my wax," he explained. "I had to lay low for a while and get my mind back in tha game." Syke nodded and began rummaging through the sacks of food. "Where's the rest of the crew?"

"I got them niggaz at the other speezy handlin' thangz," Syke replied. "Block Monsta been doin' all the cooking. I got Baby Jerk and 4 Lyfe watching over the lookouts. Being that we done turned this bitch into a full-scale operation, you can't never be too careful."

Mob appeared uninterested in what he was talking about. He quickly turned and went to sit down in the living room. "It's been some crazy shit going down, dawg," Mob stated as Young Syke dug into his food. "The word is that April is behind all of this new dope that's been flooding the streets."

"How tha fuck she do that?"

"From what I was told Plocko been giving that bitch the grade A work, while we get flooded with the mid-grade. That would explain why niggaz been flockin' elsewhere to get on, our dope ain't shit."

Young Syke mobbed into the living room and sat down across from Mob.

"That's some crazy shit, fam-o. How the plug gon' be frontin' Slim's ex-bitch some work?"

"That was my point exactly. And besides, she ain't never been really down for the homie. She always had a hidden agenda. I tried to warn Slim that she was only out for his paper, but Blood wouldn't listen. That's probably why he is where he is now."

Young Syke shook his head in disgust and said, "I wish I could murder that hoe, right fuckin' now! She keeps way too much shit going on. So now that we know who's behind the T.O. dope what we 'bout to do? It ain't like Plocko is fixin' to hand that bitch over. I wouldn't be surprised if he was fuckin' that hoe."

Mob rubbed his hands together and took a deep breath. "He probably is," he sighed. "That's why I plan to cop a few more times, playing the situation like everything is cool, then body that disloyal muthafucka too!"

"You talkin' 'bout killin' tha plug?"

Mob looked at him sideways and snarled, "*We,* my nigga. *We*—gon' kill tha plug. I done already knocked off his right-hand man, so everything is already in motion."

Young Syke seemed to be troubled by this new bit of information. "But do you think he thinks it was us?"

"I'm way too smart to leave behind any clues. I covered my trail so that no one would ever expect it was me."

"That's some super x-rated shit right there, fam-o. We 'bout to murk tha plug over a snitchin' ass bitch. What we gon' do to keep the money flowing?"

"The same thing everyone else is doing. Find another plug."

"But, where?"

"*Anywhere!* Just like other muthafuckas can do it, we can do it, too. Look, we in too deep to be actin' scared now. We just gon' have to figure this shit out as it comes to us. And if we can't come up with nothin' else—we'll just have to lay low until an opportunity presents itself."

Young Syke sat quiet trying to process what the near future would consist of. "I on't know, fam-o. This shit here seems extra wild. We gon' have a million fuckin' Mexicans on our ass once we murk that nigga. They done damn near took over the Northside, so that's gon' make it even harder to lay low."

Mob couldn't help but give some thought to what Young Syke had just said. Not only would they be at war with an unimaginable number of enemigos, but they'd need to enlist some more soldiers. "I was thinking," he began saying. "Being that we're in coalition with the Steady Grinding Boyz. What do you think about bringing them in on this?"

"*Forget it!* Fuck them niggaz, fam-o. They ain't built for this type of action. Seriously, what do they know about puttin' in work on this type of level?"

Mob shrugged. "What do any of us know? But I can say one thang for sure—them niggas gon' buss, and they'll add to our much-needed numbers. I figure if we cut them in on a small percentage—"

"Whoa—ezzz up, fam-o. Ain't that what you always tell me? First, you made them niggaz officially down with the Crimson Mafia, now you tryin' to cut them fools in our dough. Ain't no way that shit sound right. Whatchu' think they gon' do once they help us rob the connect?" Syke got up and went back into the dining room. What Mob was inquiring was too much for him to handle.

"Know that I done thought about all of that," Mob assured. "But, if them niggaz ever try to cross that line then we'll deal with they ass accordingly."

Syke opened his container and shuffled his food around. He'd clearly lost his appetite, but none of that mattered to Mob. All he was concerned about was removing the opposition.

"There was something else that I needed to tell you about," Mob continued. "The night that you were robbed, I need you to tell me that story one more time."

Syke dropped his fork and looked at Mob in utter disbelief. "I can't believe you, blood. You told me to forget about that shit. You tol' me that Poncho crushed tha nigga that robbed me in broad daylight."

120

Mob's nostrils flared as he replied, "I know what tha fuck I told you. And I still stand on anything that I said that happened. It's just that, I saw someone that looked like the cat I was in a shootout with the day Poncho was killed."

"So, what does that got to do with anything?"

"That nigga was tha Feds! I saw him and some broad meet up with two Agents this morning. I wouldn't have even noticed him if he hadn't almost run into my shit. If it weren't for that badass bitch that was with him, I'd have probably got on some bullshit. Shorty hopped out swangin' them hips, and that's when I noticed dude. But he ain't look like he did the last time I saw him. I can't say right off what's changed about him, but I know it's the same guy."

Syke picked up his fork and started eating again. "I don't know nothing about no Feds, fam-o. The niggaz I was fuckin' wit' was thorough. We was back to back bussin' at them Eastside niggaz. The only time I ever met a Federal Agent was the day I woke up in the hospital."

Mob appeared to be in deep thought. He ran one hand over his face and sighed loudly. He recalled everything Syke had told him about the Agent that was in his hospital room He also recalled everything that happened the day Poncho was murdered. If Poncho had killed a Federal Agent that day, there was no way they'd still be on the streets.

"Whatever you say," Mob conceded. "But I still need you to tell me everything you can remember about the night that you got robbed. Regardless of whether or not them niggaz was thorough—I still need to be sure."

***

Lil Menace walked out of Terisa's apartment with his mind set on revenge. When Young Syke had threatened his pistol on him unbeknownst to him he'd hammered the nail in his own coffin. Lil' Menace's every waking moment had been spent trying to devise a plan to get even. Now that he'd finally had all the pieces to the puzzle in place it was time to put everything in motion.

"What it do, cuz?" Lil' Menace greeted Crazy Cuz who sat parked in front of Terisa's apartment.

"I don't know, you tell me," Crazy Cuz replied through his partially cracked window. "You called me and told me to come over here, remember? I had plans to chill with my bitch tonight. The way you sounded when you called, I figured this was important."

Lil Menace bobbed his head up and down then held up a blunt. "You tryin' to smoke?" Crazy Cuz hit the locks and motioned for him to get in. Although tension had been at an all-time high between the two of them, Crazy Cuz was one of only a few that Lil' Menace could count on.

"How you feel about that shit that went down with Mob?" Menace inquired.

"Ain't no way we can let that shit slide. Ain't no telling who was outside and watched everything that happened."

Crazy Cuz lit the blunt Lil' Menace had given him, then snuggled into his seat. "What else is there to think? Them niggaz caught us slippin' and we paid the price for it."

Lil Menace bobbed his head in agreement. "I think we should slide through and dump on them fools. I've been thinkin' 'bout that shit nonstop since it happened. I just wanted to know what some of the homies think?"

Crazy Cuz looked at him sideways and said, "Tha fuck do you mean, what I think? I'm cut from a cloth that don't stretch. When a bitch gets outta' line it's mandatory that that nigga get puts in his place."

"But what about Big Crip? Cuz, be always on some peace treaty shit. I'm thinkin' we should get at them niggaz like, Asap! The longer we hold off on doing it, the harder it's gon' be."

Crazy Cuz pondered his suggestion for a moment while gazing out into the parking lot. It was a cold and gloomy day. The thought to retaliate had no doubt been on his mind, but out of respect for Big Crip's instructions, he simply decided to let things be. "I don't know," he admitted solemnly. "If tha big homie thinks it's best to chill then that's probably the right thing to do."

Lil Menace smirked and snipped out the remainder of the blunt in the ashtray. "You startin' to sound like that nigga, cuz. First, you was from a cloth that don't stretch, now you on some stop the violence shit."

Crazy Cuz gave him a disapproving once over and said, "You gon' keep runnin' off at the mouth until I give you what you lookin' fo' ain't chu'?"

Lil Menace laughed forcefully. "Don't play a game with yourself like that. You know what it is with me, playboy. Anytime you ready to take it there just let me know cause I stay ready." Menace snaked his hand down inside of his coat as if he were strapped.

"All that fakin' like you gon' pull ya little pistol don't faze me, cuz. I'm an Eastside muthafuckin' Grinder and I don't fear no one or nothing."

Lil Menace eyed him with a devilish smirk and said, "That's why I fucks with you, loc. This gangsta shit is in us, not on us."

Crazy Cuz gritted on him, then turned to peer out into the street. Menace was right, retaliation was a must. "It's whatever, my nigga," he spoke menacingly while gazing out into the parking lot. "I knew what it was when I got put on tha set. Grip or die." Finally, he turned and looked Lil Menace dead in the eye. "But you ain't fixin' to keep fakin' like you ready to take it there. Either we gon' do this or we're not."

Lil Menace burst into laughter once again and said, "Nigga, ain't nobody thinkin' 'bout pullin' some heat on you. I was reachin' for my phone, see?" He dug into his coat pocket and pulled out his phone.

Crazy Cuz shook his head and quickly snatched the blunt out of the ashtray.

"So, what's the plan? Now that you done talked me into

doing this crazy shit, I know you must got a plan already figured out."

Lil Menace slumped down in his seat to get comfortable again. "I'm thinkin' I should holla at Bang and fill him in on what's going down. After I get done talkin' to him, then I'll get at C-Loc, then we'll all meet up and make this shit happen."

Crazy Cuz fell silent while processing what Menace had just told him. "What Bang gotta' do with Grinder business?"

Lil Menace looked at him as if he should have already known that answer. "If cuz wanna grind with Grinders, then he gon' put in work like a Grinder. Crip or die."

"Crip or muthafuckin' die," Crazy Cuz replied.

Chapter 14

New Hope

Thursday After Work

"Faster," Derrick told himself as he raced around the track inside the fitness center. His lungs burned as he willed himself to run faster. All he could think about was the promise he'd made to his wife and son. He'd kill everyone that had something to do with their death. Although April had sworn that she'd lead him to the people that were responsible, Derrick had made up his mind that she'd be better off dead as well.

As Derrick neared his finishing point, he slowed down to a trot. He walked along the track while peering up into the ceiling, trying to catch his breath.

"Hey!" Cynthia called out from behind. "So, it's okay to just take off and leave me walking by myself?"

Derrick softly laughed and stopped to allow her time to catch up. "My bad," he said. "I wasn't trying to leave you. I always do a sprint to cap off a five-mile run."

Cynthia squinted her eyes as if she weren't going for it. "You could've at least warned me," she replied snidely.

"I did! Didn't I tell you that I go hard?" Cynthia stopped and put her hands on her hips. That was her signature move when she really got pissed. "Okay-okay, I'm sorry, alright? Partners, right?"

Cynthia rolled her eyes and brushed right past him. "Whatever," she joked. "So, what are we about to do now? Do you wanna start doing pushups and situps, or—"

"Actually, I figured we'd walk a few more laps and call it a night."

Cynthia looked confused. "Why so early? Does somebody have some secret plans for this evening that they're not talking about?"

Derrick smirked and dismissed her statement with the swat

of his hand. "Not hardly," he assured her. "I made plans to go outta town this weekend and I haven't done anything that I was supposed to have done."

"Like what?"

"Pack, I haven't packed one single suitcase yet. I've made all these plans to leave but I'm like totally unprepared to go anywhere."

They walked in silence for a while before Cynthia finally spoke. "Might I ask, where you're going?"

Derrick shook his head. Cynthia was too damn nosey. She always wanted to know everything outside of minding her own business. "I don't know," he lied.

"I'm just going somewhere so I can spend some time alone."

Cynthia peered up at him with a knowing smirk and said, "You're going outta town this weekend but you don't know where you're going?"

"Yeah! And what's with the twenty-one questions?"

"I'm just being a friend and trying to make sure that you'll be alright."

Derrick looked at her skeptically. At times, Cynthia would say things that made him think she and Georgette had discussed his past. "Have you thought about going to see your parents?" Cynthia went on to ask.

"See, that's like question number twenty-two."

"It's a simple question! If you don't want me to ask you anymore questions, then fine! We can finish these last few laps and call it a night."

Derrick's eyes slightly bulged at her response. Sure, he'd been a little evasive by not giving a straightforward answer, but he never thought that it would upset her. "Look, this is not something you should be getting all mad about. I just don't like talking about my parents. As soon as you brought them up, I instantly started thinking about how mad at me they are." Derrick looked away to appear consumed with what was going on on the handball court.

"Whatever was done is done," Cynthia reminded him. "Sooner or later your parents are gonna have to let the past go so that y'all can be a family again."

Derrick laughed forcefully. "Sounds like a good dream you're having. My parents are too caught up in being holier than thou to be concerned with being a family. In their eyes, they don't make mistakes. God forgives, but they don't."

Cynthia nodded, yet remained silent. She knew all too well what he was dealing with, as well as the only way he could fix it. "Somehow this conversation has turned and gone down the wrong road," Cynthia said apologetically. "I didn't mean to cause all those hurtful memories to resurface."

Derrick waved her off and said, "It's not your fault that my life is in the shape that it is. This is just the cards that I was dealt. This entire week you've done nothing but somehow put my mind in a better place. I can't remember the last time I went out and had as much fun as I did that night. You're the reason I've been at ease here lately. And you're the only person that I really have to talk to with all that said, you haven't done anything wrong. In my book, you've done everything just right."

Cynthia blushed, she never thought Derrick appreciated her efforts to say something as heartfelt as that. "Awww," she cooed unconsciously reaching to take his hand. "That was sooo sweet!" Derrick stopped walking and stare down at his hand. "What?" she asked looking confused.

Derrick lifted his arm and said, "Do you mind if I have my hand back?"

Cynthia's eyes fluttered. "Boy!" She snatched her hand away from him and began to walk away. "Don't nobody wanna hold your sweaty ass hands, anyway. I don't know why you grabbed my hand."

"Oh, I grabbed your hand?" he yelled out after her. "I think you've got that all twisted around. You grabbed my hand!"

***

1:30 A.M.

Stacks on top of stacks of paperwork lay scattered about the dining room table. Detailed reports that gave times, dates, names, and places of drug transactions. Agent Stevens worked until the wee hours of the morning trying to figure out who the female's voice was that he'd heard over the wiretaps. Whoever she was, she had to be schooled in the game to be as elusive as she was. But as he sat staring at an old file that detailed how Slim had used April as a mule, he became concerned that that might be the case now. Was there some major supplier forcing a helpless young woman to work for them?

"Honey, how long will you be sitting in here going over those same reports?" Stevens turned to see his wife of thirty-two years standing behind him.

"I have just a few more things that I'd like to go over and then I'll come to bed." Stevens removed his reading glasses and peered up at her with a gentle smile. "I promise this shouldn't take too much longer."

Margaret sauntered across the room over to where he sat holding firm to the file that he'd been reading. "What's this that you're reading?" she asked, then bent down to peer eagerly over his shoulder.

Stevens snapped the file shut and carelessly tossed it into the center of the table. "You know I can't allow you to read any of that," he said seriously. "Why would you ask me something crazy like that?"

Margaret wrapped her arms around him in a loving embrace. "Because I want to know what's so important that has my husband up at all times of the night. You've been so consumed with work that you've got into the habit of letting life just pass you by." She stepped around in front of him to sit in his lap.

"We've raised three beautiful children and have four adorable grandchildren as a result. Is Slim and his bunch of drug smuggling hooligans worth you missing our grandkids grow up?"

Stevens sighed, feeling the slight sting of resentment. He'd worked his ass off to become a DEA Agent. It was because of his hard work that enabled his family to enjoy the life they'd lived. But as he sat there thinking about it, reality finally settled in. It wasn't the money that had turned their old house into a home, it was the unwavering love that they all expressed toward one another.

Stevens pulled his wife closer and hugged her tightly. He couldn't help but think how foolish he was to think that money could buy what he had. "You're right," he admitted and rested his head against her bosom. "Nothing is worth me missing our grandchildren grow up."

Margaret lifted his head so that she could peer into his eyes. "Well, let's go," she spoke softly. "You've already given this job all of your youth. What more can anyone ask of you? I need my husband back. I want to grow old together and watch our grandchildren grow up and have children of their own."

Stevens smile and looked at his wife with all the love and admiration that was humanly possible. "I give you my word," he began saying. "Once I finish with this case, I'm done! I'll retire and we can go and do whatever your heart so desires."

Margaret closed her eyes and shook her head. She fought desperately to find the words that would describe the terrible emptiness that she suddenly felt inside.

"What's wrong?" Stevens asked, noting the sour expression etched on his wife's face. "I really need to know that you're on board with this thing."

Margaret sighed and laid her forehead against his and said, "If you don't walk away from this thing now, then you never will."

***

A man sat alone in his cell gazing intently into the shadowy darkness.

Although his eyes were trained on a dark corner in his cell, he saw far beyond the concrete walls that he was confined in. Somehow his mind's eye was transfixed on how his near future would unfold.

Slim stood, stretching to relieve the ever-growing anxiety building inside him. He caught movement in the mirror that was mounted to the wall and moved closer to inspect the image staring back at him.

"Who are you?" the question rolled off his lips as if he were talking to someone else in the room.

Although he was of sound mind and body, the person he saw staring back at him appeared weak. Quickly growing frustrated at the mere sight of himself, he began to pace. His future looked bleak, no doubt. But to say he'd never see freedom again, had yet to be determined.

Shortly after his short exercise of pacing back and forth, Slim retired to his bunk for some much-needed rest. Tomorrow morning, he was scheduled to meet with his new attorney, David Longborrow. If everything went as planned, this might be the break that he'd been looking for. He'd already fired two attorneys because of their inability to handle the pressure. He needed someone with resources, someone that wasn't afraid to fight, someone that was confident in the job that they did, and willing to do whatever it takes to win. The only way Slim would ever see the light of day again was if the man he was about to meet could fit those shoes.

The next morning, Slim was awakened by two County Officials there to escort him to his visit. Instantly his stomach began to churn at the idea of the endless possibilities that lie ahead. Everything that he'd hoped for came down to this very moment. Slim's family spoke highly of the new attorney that was there to see him. All he could hope for now was that everything they'd told him was true.

Slim was led into a small room and handcuffed to the table across from his new attorney. He sat quietly observing the older white man as he scribbled line after line onto a yellow legal pad. Judging by the way he was dressed, Slim could only assume that the man was confident and well established. He wore an expensive Italian suit with a gold watch peeking from beneath the sleeve. He was bald just like Slim, except he wore a neatly trimmed reddish-white beard. He seemed completely oblivious to the fact that Slim had entered the room and was now sitting in front of him.

"Excuse me," Slim said kindly imploring for the man's attention. "Can't all of that wait until this meeting is over?"

David Longborrow peered up at Slim over the rim of his glasses. "I apologize for the wait," he said. "But if you'll be so kind as to give me one more second, I'll be done with this rather quickly."

Slim glared at the man as he continued to jot down line after line into his legal pad. Slim had tons of things that he was ready to discuss, and because of that, his patience was wearing thin. "Peep game, fam. I didn't have my family pay you all that money just so you could come in here and work on somebody else's shit. This time is on my dime. If you don't mind, I'ma need you to put all that up so we can talk about my case."

David Longborrow calmly set his pin on the table and leaned back in his chair. He crossed his legs at the knee and tossed his wire-rimmed glasses on his legal pad. "Mr. Lewis, I'm the one that decides when *my* hourly rate begins, not you. And secondly, you're not the only person in America that can afford an attorney. Just because I told the guards to go and get you, doesn't mean that I have to stop what I'm doing just as soon as you walk in the door."

Slim glared at his new attorney with a look that could kill and said, "Yeah, but I paid for you to be here. If you had other things you needed to get done, then you should've done that shit before you got here."

David Longborrow forced a weak smile. He knew how badly Slim needed good representation. All this bickering he was doing was just a sign of how anxious he was. "So, tell me,

Mr. Lewis. What is it that you think I can do for you?"

Slim chuckled and spoke softly, "The audacity of this muthafucka." He crossed his legs at the knee mimicking his attorney. "First of all, for one hundred and thirty grand you should be telling *me* what you can do. And secondly, don't get this little situation of me being locked up twisted like niggaz can't still be touched. I'm a fool about my chedda. If you don't wanna play by the rules, then I won't either."

David Longborrow chuckled and said, "*The audacity of this muthafucka.* Don't let this old white man dressed in a suit fool ya. This shit right here—" He pointed down at Slim's file. "I do this for a living. They'll lock your ass up for eternity if you ever threaten me again."

Both men shared a brief staredown, neither of them was willing to break eye contact. But with David Longborrow being a man that was about his business, he'd never allow a misunderstanding to come between his money. "The case can't be bought," he spoke seriously. "That little thirty thousand that you tacked on won't do anything but make you the laughingstock of the courtroom. The Federal Government are the ones that make the money that you're so willing to toss around. I expect if you ever plan to be a free man again, you'll come up with a better plan than trying to buy the case."

Slim almost smiled, he couldn't have asked for a better response. Not only had this new attorney just proved to be exactly the type of lawyer he'd been looking for, but he knew all too well how to read between the lines.

"The extra cash wasn't to try and buy the case," Slim informed him. "There are some very important things that I'd like for you to do with that money."

David Longborrow appeared to give it some thought, "Oh, yeah, like what?"

"Like, get me outta this segregated housing unit that I'm being housed in. I should be in general population like everyone else. I haven't done anything that would justify them housing me in here. They're just trying to limit my access to the streets."

"As they should, it says here that you're a menace to society."

Slim laughed. "You of all people should know that that's the label that they give all black people."

David chuckled. "So, this is another case about a black man being falsely accused?"

"You hit it right on the money. Those snake muthafuckas got me charged with trafficking but they ain't got shit on me. The place where I got jammed up ain't where I live. I don't own that dusty ass piece of shit. The only thing that connects me to that place is my truck."

David Longborrow thumbed through several papers until he found what he was looking for. "Conspiracy to traffic cocaine, first Degree murder—"

"That charge got dropped! And like I said, they didn't catch me doing nothing. Whatever they found in that place belongs to the people that own it. I was just visiting."

"Who?"

"A friend! What difference does it make who I was there to see? All I know is, I was talking to a friend of mine and then *boom*! The door came flying in. The next thing I knew the place was swarming with masked men yelling, *"Get Down!"* I was so spooked that I ran out the back door and took off into the woods."

"And what happened next?"

Slim shrugged. "They caught me. They chased me down and cuffed me and that's why I'm here having this conversation with you now."

"I see. So, what about the extra thirty grand that you paid me? You still haven't explained to me what that was for."

Slim glanced back at the door and inched closer to the table. "I need a cell phone," he spoke softly. "I have some important people that I need to speak to, but I can't do it using their phone. And the guys that's on my case, I'd like for you to put a couple of grand on their books so that they're comfortable. You know that pressure busts pipes and these bitch ass muthafuckas don't have no problem with applying it."

David Longborrow went on to scribble line after line onto his yellow legal pad. Slim was almost certain that he'd say something about the ex, April but surprisingly he didn't.

"I'll see what I can do about getting you back in general population, no later than this evening," David Longborrow went on to say. "And if you continue to have problems after you're moved back in population, make sure to give me a call." He smiled.

Slim nodded in understanding already knowing what he was implying. Not only did that smile say that he'd soon have everything he'd asked for, but the fight for his freedom had just begun.

Chapter 15

Weekend Get Away

Nothing could compare to the utmost feeling of gratitude that Derrick felt as he gazed over the waves on South Beach. He'd never beheld such a beautiful sight. April had gone above and beyond to ensure that he was in want of nothing when he arrived at the airport.

"Mr. Walker?" A middle-aged white man greeted him, holding up a sign with Derrick's name on it.

Derrick gave the man a once over and looked around to see if April was somewhere near. "Yeah, that's me," he replied, forcing a smile. "Who are you?"

"My name is, Tony," the man replied as he extended his hand for a handshake. "Ms. Jordan sent me to pick you up and take you out to where you'll be staying."

Derrick appeared a little uneasy about this. He'd warned April that their meeting would have to remain a secret. If anything looked suspicious, he'd swore to her that he'd leave. "Where's April?"

"She's already waiting for you at the place where you'll be staying. Now if you will—I'll take these." He reached and grabbed Derrick's bags but he was still a little reluctant to let go. Sure, his gut warned him not to go through with this, but the only way to find the people that had killed his family was to take a chance.

Derrick was whisked away to a secluded area out on South Beach. The mere sight of the beautiful beach house where he'd be staying instantly done away with any ill thoughts. He anxiously peered through the windows of the limousine trying to take in the massive home. He'd expected to see April somewhere in the mist waiting for him, but as the car came to a stop, he began to feel that she wasn't around.

"And here it is!" Tony exclaimed as he held open the door for Derrick to get out. "Ms. Jordan also instructed me to give you this when you arrived."

He handed Derrick a small envelope and said, "You'll need to use this code to get in the front door."

"But—why should I have to use a code if she's already here?"

Tony shrugged and popped the trunk. "Change of plans. I spoke with her briefly on the way here. She told me to tell you that she'll be here in a minute."

Derrick peered down at the envelope, then back up at Tony. "So, you're just gonna leave me here to figure all this out on my own?"

Tony laughed and handed him his duffel bag and said, "I'm sure you're in good hands. My advice to you is, go in there and try to relax. From what I can see, Ms. Jordan went through a lot of trouble to make sure that you're alright."

The memory of how uneasy he'd felt the first day that he'd arrived made Derrick laugh. Why he was so worried about something that was obviously so well thought out was beyond his wildest dreams. But as he stood looking at the waves roll on to the beach, he couldn't help but remember what it felt like when he stepped inside the house.

"This shit is off tha chain," he uttered softly and dropped his bag on the floor.

The living room walls were made up of floor to ceiling windows. From the comfort of that one room, he could almost see the entire beach. By the time he'd finally made it around to checking out the master bedroom, he thought surely that there'd be nothing else. Outside of the splendid views and exquisite decor, what more should he have to expect? Regardless of what April may have told him about not needing to bring any clothes, nothing could prepare him for what he saw next.

Bags on top of bags lay scattered about the bedroom floor. Everything from Gucci to Armani spilled from the bags purposely. Derrick carefully waded through April's suitcases until he'd reached the bed. A note lay on top of a box of

Yeezy's shoes, conspicuously placed in the center of the bed.

I hope you like all the clothes that I bought for you. You wouldn't 1believe everything that I had to go through to get your sizes. ☺ *I'll be back at the house shortly. Get dressed and be ready to go out and get something to eat. I left something special for you on top of the dresser. I hope you like it. Kisses. Talk to you soon, April!*

Derrick turned and saw several boxes of jewelry on top of the dresser. *The jewelry, the beach house, the clothes were all too much,* he thought. There was no way she could legitimately afford this type of lifestyle unless her hands were involved in something illegal.

Derrick thought back to something April had said over a year ago, *"I stole a quarter-million dollars from Slim and that's why all these people are trying to kill me."*

That revelation alone echoed over and over in his mind. Surely the money she'd taken had long since been gone. So, how could she afford to splurge like this?

Derrick took a deep breath to try and steady his thoughts. Everything April had done for him was without question appreciated, but it all came at what cost? Before, just a simple affair had cost him every one that he loved. And now that he'd made the decision to tango with the devil again. What would it cost him now?

"What are you doing out here?" April asked as she stepped out onto the patio behind him. Derrick never said a word, he calmly swirled his glass of liquor around and took a sip. "Did I miss something?"

Derrick smirked. "Nah, you didn't miss nothing," he assured her. "I'm sure that you already know, I've got a few things on my mind."

April's expression slightly softened as she snuggled up beside him. "Things like what?"

"How can you afford all of this? Seriously—it's not like you're some high paid attorney working at a big law firm. And I know damn well you didn't hit the lottery. So, what's going on? Are you back messing around with another big-time drug dealer?"

April dismissed his assumption with the wave of her hand. "I never told you that I didn't have a job. You just assumed I didn't. My idea of employment is much more different than yours. And besides, where is all of this coming from?"

Derrick looked her dead in the eye when he sensed how evasive she was being. "Take a wild guess," he replied sarcastically. "After everything, I've been through you don't think that I *deserve* to know what you're up to?"

"It's not that I don't feel you deserve to know. The real question is, do you *need* to know. Is all this negative energy that I'm feeling because you wanna' know how I make a living?"

"Negative energy? Don't misconstrue my unwillingness to be left alone in the dark with acting negative. I fully understand what comes with this type of lifestyle. I mean, look at us." He gestured to what she wore but was suddenly rendered speechless.

The dress that she wore left little to the imagination. She was completely naked underneath. She'd been the object of temptation since their weekend together had begun. He'd stood strong against most of her advancements at the beginning. He'd stood strong even when she'd climbed into the shower with him. He'd stood strong against practically everything, but when he'd woke up one morning with his dick in her mouth, he punished her.

"What about us?" April asked snidely. "That cheap bottle of Crown must got you seeing things. I bought us nothing but the finest."

Derrick shook his head and replied, "That isn't what I'm talking about. All I was saying was—"

"You don't appreciate nothing," she chimed in.

"That's not it either."

"In so many words it's got to be. I flew you out to this beautiful place on the beach, bought you everything you needed. And this attitude is how you repay me?"

Derrick looked away and said, "I didn't ask for any of this April. I came here to find out about the people that killed my family. You promised you'd tell me about them, yet you've avoided that conversation every time I've asked about them."

"I avoided it because I didn't wanna ruin our weekend."

"Ruin it for who—*me*?" Derrick laughed forcefully and said, "You must've forgot that my life was already ruined. Sounds like you're still caught up in the moment. Ain't that how all this shit started? Us being caught up in the moment?"

April turned to peer out over the beach. He was right, he deserved to know the truth. She was reluctant to share certain bits of information out of fear of being judged by him. "What do you say if we go down by the water and finish having this conversation?"

"See there you go," Derrick said. "You're always looking for a way out of doing what you said you'd do."

April peered up at him and said, "There's only one way out of this situation. That much I'm certain of. I figured since our plane leaves in a few hours. Why not walk the beach and talk before we left?" Derrick appeared a little skeptical about her idea so to squash all doubts. She said, "Everything that you've been waiting to hear, I'll happily tell you. I just wanted to feel the sand between my toes one last time before we go."

It didn't take long for Derrick to make up his mind that he'd join her for a walk along the beach. After all, the whole reason he was there was to listen to what she had to say.

The white sand beach was an amazing sight to see. Brilliant shades of yellow, splashed over burnt orange gave the announcement that sunset was upon them. Tall palm trees swayed back and forth in the distance, while exotic birds graced the sky.

"April!" Derrick called out while trailing from a short distance behind her. "I thought we were supposed to talk?"

April stopped and looked back at him. Although her eyes were concealed by dark tinted glasses it was obvious that something was troubling her. "We are going to talk," she replied. "But isn't this just beautiful?" She turned to peer out over the waves again, forced to remove her hair from over her face because of the wind.

"It's nice, but this view isn't why I decided to come have a walk with you. Don't get me wrong, the clothes, the jewelry, the house—all is great! Your generosity is unmatched, but you promised we'd talk so I'm listening."

April sauntered down closer by the water, so close that the water was now rolling on top of her feet. "Have you ever wanted someone dead so bad that you were willing to do anything to make sure that it happened?"

Derrick pulled his dreadlocks back and tied them together. "What kind of question is that April? What does me wanting someone dead have to do with you?"

"Everything. The people I'm connected to are very powerful people. They're the kind of people that you may need to have in your corner someday."

Derrick shook his head and replied, "They can't do nothing for me. My business is legit. I don't sell drugs, nor do I have any desire to. I don't need their money, protection, or anything else they might have to offer."

"What if they could lead you to the people that killed your family?"

This was the part of the weekend he'd been waiting for. It took everything inside of Derrick not to reveal how anxious he was to hear what she had to say. "So, I guess you're going to introduce me to these people, huh? Or, should I look forward to continuing to figure this crazy situation out on my own? You keep dangling bits and pieces of information over my head. Why not just spit it out? Say what you've got to say so we can start figuring out what the next step is going to be."

"Truthfully, I haven't decided if I'm going to introduce you to them or not. One of the people I'm involved with there's no way in hell you'll ever meet him. And the other's—well, we'll just have to put our heads together and come up with a plan."

Derrick nodded approvingly as he too walked down closer by the water. Although April was finally talking, there was so much that he still needed to know but for some reason, she was still being reluctant to tell him.

"So, what's the catch?" Derrick asked. "You're talking to me like you're trying to negotiate a deal. Instead of laying everything on the table that you're holding back."

"I'm holding back because you're being too hostile. Things are fixing to get a little hectic and the last person that I need flipping the script on me is you."

Derrick chuckled softly. "Well, I can agree to tone down my attitude, but you've gotta quit bullshittin' and keep it all the way one hunnit."

April smiled and crossed her arms, leaning in for a kiss. "A deal is a deal and it's sealed with a kiss."

Adrian Dulan

Chapter 16

Retaliation Is A Must

Lil' Menace stood in Terisa's breezeway fuming because Bang hadn't returned any of his calls. He'd called him several times throughout the day only to be forwarded to his voice mail as if he were one of his side chicks. Not only had Bang failed to be available like his position required him to be, but that night Menace had plans to make him an official member of his set.

Menace took a long hard pull from his blunt while he stood pondering everything he could think about Bang. His style, the way he dressed, the weird things he said. Something about him didn't add up. He wasn't a thorough street nigga like everyone else he was accustomed to dealing with. No one from the hood had ever heard of him either. In fact, the more Menace tried to figure out who he was, the more his mind was being made up. If Bang wanted to live to see another day, he'd have to earn his stripes and become a Steady Grinding Boy.

Headlights lit up the breezeway casting light on Menace as he stood concealed by darkness. Judging by the color of the SUV it was Bang. Lord only knows how he knew where Lil Menace was at. Lil Menace made a mental note to ask him about it when they spoke.

"Where tha' fuck you been, cuz?" Menace emerged from the breezeway in an all-black hooded coat. He cautiously scanned up and down the parking lot as Bang hopped out and approached him.

"My bad," Bang replied. "I got caught up trying to handle a little business. By the time I was finished, my girl needed to use the truck. I'm sure you know how that story goes. Even though they say they'll only be gone for an hour them crazy hoes be gone all day!"

Lil Menace hit his blunt again as he steadily drew closer. His dark blue dickies dragged along the concrete causing him to have to pull them up. "What tha fuck does yo' bitch gotta do with me? Matter of fact, what does anything you've been doing today have to do with me?"

Bang looked confused. "I was just—"

"Ain't no, *I was just*! When I call, you answer. Didn't the big homie tell you how this shit was supposed to play out? You told us you could handle the position, didn't you?"

"I did, and I can. I just let my girl use the fuckin' truck. She—"

"Nigga, fuck dat! Ain't nobody tryin' to hear that sob story, cuz. If I gotta blow yo' phone up before you decide to answer we gon' have some problems."

Bang looked away on that note. He was tired of playing the role of a weakling to people that he could easily snap into pieces. He was a trained DEA Agent. Trained to shoot. Trained to kill. "It won't happen again," he spoke sternly, eyeing Lil Menace with the same intensity that he looked upon him with. "What was so important that you called me for, anyway? I know that it had to be something serious because you're trippin' out on me over nothing."

Lil Menace forcefully chuckled. He scanned the parking lot one more time and said, "Nigga, who tha fuck you think you talkin' to cuz?"

Bang had to check his temper and make sure that he kept it in check. "I wasn't trying to offend you, I was just saying."

"Just saying?" Menace forcefully chuckled again. "How you know I was over here?"

"C-Loc I talked to him earlier and tha homie told me where you was."

"Tha homie?" Lil Menace repeated and gave Bang a thorough once over. "Nigga, you gotta earn that. C-Loc ain't cho' muthafuckin' homie. Cuz is a Grinder. If you wanna be looked at like you're official, then you gotta put that work in."

Bang nodded, feeling the tension between them quickly starting to mount. To keep things from escalating to the point of no return he cleverly tried to move the conversation along.

"You never told me what was so important," he said. "I know you called way earlier, but I'm here now. Do you need a ride somewhere, or need me to run and pick something up?"

Lil Menace smirked, sensing that Bang must've been feeling himself. Besides the fact that he stood eyeing him the same way that he looked upon him, he had a certain air of confidence. Not the kind that was confident in his looks, but the kind that said that he had the upper hand, and you just didn't know how.

"Remember that shit that went down the other day?" Lil Menace said, studying Bang ever so closely. "A couple of the homies is trying to link up and slid through there on them niggaz. Since that bitch ass nigga Syke act like he wanted to up that thang on a nigga, we gon' sho' 'em how the Eastside get down."

Bang shook his head unable to agree with what he was hearing. Not only was he unprepared, but he had no way of letting someone know what was about to go down. "I don't think that'll be a good idea," he replied, trying to sound convincing. "Do you remember how many people were in the courtyard that day? It's gonna be a massacre if we go back over there. I think you should rethink this whole situation. It's too many reasons why that plan won't work. If you called me all the way over here, just to ask me that—then I'm out." Bang turned as if he were about the head back over to his truck. He'd hoped that what he'd just said would make Lil Menace feel like his plan was ridiculous, but it didn't.

"Who said I was askin'?" Menace spat, stopping Bang dead in his tracks. "I'm tellin' you how this shit is about to go down. Either you gon' ride tonight, or you gon' die tonight. My heater can either go ham on you or tha ops." Lil Menace pulled out his .40 cal, allowing it dangle beside him so that Bang could see it.

Bang's gut had warned him not to show up that night, but his eagerness to find out who'd killed his partner had landed him knee-deep in a trap.

***

4 Lyfe sat posted in front of the spot serving as a lookout, while Block Monsta and Young Syke did a money count inside. Every night just before midnight they'd close down shop so that the Hill Side Courtz gang could take over. That was Young Syke's special way of allowing them to feel in control. But at the crack of dawn each day, someone from the Goon Squad would reopen shop and it'd be business as usual.

4 Lyfe sat in a chair just outside the door. No lights were shining in the breezeway so for the most part, it was utterly dark. The only lights that could be seen were the streetlamps raining down over the courtyard. 4 Lyfe's mind raced to try and figure out a way to leave unnoticed. It was only a matter of time before the Steady Grinding Boyz would be there to kill everyone. 4 Lyfe scanned the courtyard and spotted Baby Jerk walking in the distance. His job was to watch out for 12 and keep a watchful eye out for jack boyz. The rule for being a lookout was simple. Never leave your post, and if something looked suspicious— shoot first and ask questions later.

The sound of a door being slammed shut jolted 4 Lyfe out of his observations. A young teenage boy scurried into view totting a bag of trash. His crimson-colored shirt and tan khakis instantly drew 4 Lyfe's attention. Tonight, was not a good night to be still wearing his school uniform. Just by the sight of it, 4 Lyfe took that as his final warning to get out of dodge.

"Baby Jerk!" he called out, standing to leave his post. "Syke told me to handle something real quick. I need you to hold the spot down until I come back."

Baby Jerk peered back at him but never said a word. Everyone knew the rules for their position. If he was willing to gamble with his life, then who was he to stop him.

***

Bang pulled inside the Hill Side Courtz, driving an old school box Chevy. The tenants were rather quiet that night. The crisp night air had brought on a seasonal reaction. Instead of junkies roaming the courtyard in search of their next hit, everyone was inside. The only people that Bang could see were runners and people coming home for the evening.

Lil Menace sat alongside Bang navigating him through the apartments. Although Bang clearly remembered exactly where to go, Menace wanted to be sure that they had a good look at everything moving about.

"A'ight when we bend the corner up ahead try and see if you see the homie," Lil Menace instructed everyone. "Cuz is supposed to be posted up in the breezeway outside of the spot we're fixin' to hit. Syke and 'em always do a money count around this time of night so look closely so we don't miss it."

Bang made a left now driving much slower than he was before. No one was outside except a handful of addicts and a few Hill Side Courtz members and—"

Skerrrrrrrr!

"Look out!" Bang shouted, narrowly missing a young kid that had just run in front of the car.

"I bet that's one of them niggaz right there," Crazy Cuz spat as he glared at the teenage boy that now ran through the courtyard. "Cuz sportin' them tan khakis and redshirt. And look he just ran up in that breezeway where it's a nigga posted up in the dark."

Everyone's attention was drawn to the building as they crept past. There were no other apartment buildings that showed any activity except for that one.

"No soon as you hit the corner you need to hurry up and park. Them niggaz might've seen us almost hit shorty back there. We gotta make this shit quick. Hit them niggaz while they busy doin' some other shit so we can get tha fuck up outta here."

Bang turned the corner and immediately found a place to park. His hands were shaking so bad that he had to ball them into to fist hoping that no one would notice.

"Tha fuck is you trembling for?" Lil Menace quipped noticing how uneasy Bang had suddenly become. "You must thought it was a game when I told you we about to put in some work. We don't do walk-ons' on this set. Either you gon' put in some work, or you gon' get dumped on just like these bitch ass niggaz." Lil Menace chambered a slug in the barrel of his sawed-off pump. He quickly pulled his skully down just above his eyes and said, "Crazy Cuz, you and C-Loc hit the front door while me and Bang get off through the windows. Don't worry about tryin' to get the money. Let's just get in and get out. Kill everythang that you see movin'."

Bang peered over at Lil Menace confused as to what he was to do. He had no weapon, no mask, let alone the heart to kill an innocent person.

"Here you take this," Lil Menace said as he retrieved a 9mm from the glove box. "I'll let you use this for tonight. But know that if you don't empty this muthafuckin' clip, we gon' make do on what I told you."

Bang looked down at the gun he now held in his hands. It seemed crazy to think that such a small piece of steel was his only means of salvation. Either he would go through with what he was told to do, or he would die tonight.

Everyone took off through the apartment complex at a slow trot. The only sound that could be heard was the patter of their feet as they weaved in between each building. As they neared the back of the apartment building, they formed a line and placed their backs against the wall. Crazy Cuz took the lead and spared a peek into the breezeway.

"He's still there," he whispered while peering back at everyone lined up behind him. "You and Bang gon' and head around front. I'll give you one minute to get in place, then we gon' do this."

Lil Menace nodded and quickly disappeared into the night. When Crazy Cuz was certain that they'd made it in position, he spared another peek into the breezeway.

A dark figure moved about pacing from one side of the breezeway to the other. Judging by his size, Crazy Cuz could only assume that it wasn't 4 Lyfe. "Is you ready?" C-Loc nodded, but when Crazy Cuz peered back into the breezeway he was met by a blinding flurry.

Bok! Bok! Bok! Bok! Bok!

The sudden burst of gunfire sent Crazy Cuz back-peddling into C-Loc. But being that Crazy Cuz was never one to fold under pressure, he instantly retaliated.

Pldddd! Pldddd! Plddddd!

Bullets ricocheted off the stairs and ground causing the man in the breezeway to cower for cover. As soon as Crazy Cuz realized that he'd sent the man running they made a break for the front door.

Boom!

C-Loc kicked the front door in almost knocking it off its hinges. Several people wide-eyed with fear peered up at them as they ran up in the apartment. Without another moment to lose they both lined someone in their sights and let it rip.

Boom! Boom! Boom!

Bullets tore through their bodies dropping them dead where they were.

Before C-Loc and Crazy Cuz even realized what they'd done an entire family lay riddled with bullets in front of them.

"Fuck!" Frantically they searched from face to face hoping to find at least one Crimson Mafia member. When reality finally settled in that they'd made a terrible mistake Crazy Cuz peered over at C-Loc and said, "Let's get outta' here. We just hit the wrong apartment!"

They took off back through the complex meeting up with Bang and Lil Menace who was already at the car. Just as they all piled inside, and Bang started the car the sound of a hailstorm caused them all to cringe.

Boom! Doom! Cooom! Poom! Boom!

"Drive this muthafucka!" Lil Menace yelled while ducking low in his seat to keep from getting hit. Now instead of creeping through an apartment complex that utterly felt like a ghost town, the entire place was suddenly buzzing with action. Hill Side niggaz dipped through cuts aiming and shooting at them.

Bang slammed on the gas pedal causing the engine to roar to life. The tires squealed, the rear end swerved, sparks flew as they scraped over speed bumps. Hill Side niggaz were relentless in their assault. Several goons chased behind them in a vain attempt to overcome them.

C-Loc swung his arm out the window hoping that he could hold them off. But right before he squeezed, he was hit by enemy gunfire.

"Ah-hhhh!" he howled in pain and fell back into the seat. Lil Menace spared a peek over the seat checking to see how bad he was injured. C-Loc didn't look good, blood soiled the front of his sweatshirt. If they didn't get him out of there quickly, they'd all meet the same fate.

Skerrrrrr! The Chevys tires clawed at the pavement as they sped out of the complex. At any moment the entire area would be crawling with police. Bang couldn't be caught dead in a situation like this. There was an apartment full of dead people behind them and he was the getaway driver of the people responsible for doing it. Regardless of him being a DEA Agent, the Press would have a field day with that story.

"Where tha fuck is you going?" Lil Menace replied, noting that Bang had turned out of the complex and began driving the wrong direction.

"I'm trying to get us outta here," Bang fired back. "Chill, there's nothing but dirt roads and highway up ahead. If we drive back towards the Eastside, we'll surely get—" Two County cruisers sped down the opposite side of the street headed straight towards them. Bang slowed down and tried to blend in with traffic praying that they'd be overlooked. But with bullet holes speckled all over the car, their prayers were only wishful thinking.

"Go-go-go!" Crazy Cuz shouted, watching in horror as

both vehicles busted a U-turn in the middle of the street. But no matter how good of a driver Bang was the old school box Chevy was no match for the police cruisers equipped with modern-day technology.

Crazy Cuz grabbed C-Loc's Ar-15 and used the butt of it to knock out the shattered back window. Both cruisers were gradually gaining on them so Crazy Cuz had to remain patient until the right moment.

Plllllldddd! Pllldddd! Pldddddddd!

The windshield on the first cruiser buckled as slugs punched holes through it. The driver never had a chance. Slugs hammered into the driver's side sending the car crashing into on-coming traffic.

Boom!

"No-no-no!" Bang exclaimed while slamming his fist into the steering wheel. "You don't kill the fuckin' police. If you shoot tha fuckin' cops they'll stop at nothing until we're all dead!" Everyone seemingly paused for a moment and glared at him, had they have known he too was an officer he'd have been on the other end of Crazy Cuz's barrel.

"Nigga, you don't shut tha fuck up and just drive, we gon' put yo' bitch ass out there so you can be with them." Lil Menace spat.

Bang ice grilled him out the corner of his eye. As much as he'd like to take him up on that offer, he couldn't. He was an accessory to murder.

Crazy Cuz lined the last cruiser up in his sights. The driver clearly knew to follow them at a safe distance. But, regardless of how far back he was, they were speeding head-on into a massacre.

Pldddddddd!

The County Cruiser veered left before making a sharp right. Just as the driver managed to regain control, *Bam!* He slammed into another car.

"Now that's how an Eastside nigga supposed to do it!" Lil Menace celebrated. "When twelve get on your heels, give them muthafuckas hell." Menace peered over at Bang who suddenly appeared distracted and said, "Welcome to the set, playboy. You a Grinder for Life now. Always put tha hood befo' everythang and you'll be a'ight."

Chapter 17

This Isn't Real

Something loud awoke Mob from another restless slumber. The noise sounded as if it were coming from a rocking chair or something wooden crackling under pressure. Mob strained to look around to find the irritating sound, but he was helpless. Both hands and feet had been hogtied behind him. His wrists burned from the rope that bound them. Each time he moved his breathing became laborious because of the duct tape that covered his mouth.

Creek! Creeek! Creek!

Mob tilted his head back as far as he could. He still couldn't see anything yet. The side of his neck was sticky and wet, possibly from dried blood. He scanned the room to try and figure out where he was, but it was empty. Not so much as one single portrait could be seen on the glowing white walls. A double door closet to his left was ajar revealing nothing but more darkness. Mob wiggled around yet a little more causing beads of sweat to build across his forehead. The more he moved about something or someone came into view. It was there by the window in a chair. Every time the chair rocked forward the light from outside gave the dark figure its features.

Creek!

It wore something long and black, the type of garment a monk or a priest would wear.

Creek!

Its face appeared to be a white mask, except it had pointy facial features. The nose was unnaturally long. Its ears too large to be human.

Maybe elfin, he thought. *Or something much more sinister like a gothic demon.*

Creeeeek!

Suddenly the chair stopped. The dark figure sat in plain view watching him. Its pointy facial features no longer had a fake costume look to it. Strangely enough, everything looked real. Mob squirmed around yet a little more, straining to get a better look. He had to be certain that what he'd saw was just that. Something he'd seen, when he'd finally managed to turn around, the dark figure leaned closer allowing him a better look and smiled.

"Mmmhhhhh!" Muffled cries of terror fought to escape the duct tape that covered Mob's mouth. He twisted his hands back and forth desperately trying to break free.

The dark figure stood from his seat and slowly crossed the room. He laughed softly at first, but gradually that laughter turned into an over-exaggerated bellow. Mob worked relentlessly to break the ropes that bound him. His breaths grew shorter and shorter as panic threatened to overcome him. Suddenly, the door to the room came crashing in. Another figure emerged from the hallway. His presence only brought on more fear and the overwhelming stench of rotting flesh.

"Mhhhhhhhh! Mmmm! Mmmhhhh!" Mob's muffled cries only excited his tormentors more.

They huddled closely around him as if they were ready to pounce. One pulled out something long and black from beneath his robe. It looked like a hammer, he raised it.

"Remember this?" he asked.

The repugnant odor that escaped his mouth caused Mob to gag. He fought desperately to subdue the vomit threatening to explode from within, but he couldn't. Vomit poured from his nostrils forcing him to swallow the rest just to breathe. One of his tormentors reached down and lifted his head, forcing him to look at him.

"We'll see if you remember this by the time we get done with you." He swung.

Splack!

Mob awoke screaming at the top of his lungs. He accidentally fell out of bed knocking everything off his nightstand. Panic surged through his mind as he laid looking around his bedroom. This was the place that he still called home, but something about it felt strangely different.

The alarm clock suddenly went off startling him. Mob quickly scooped it up fumbling at the buttons until he'd managed to shut it off. He took a few deep breaths to try and calm his nerves. He made himself think of normal things, things that he was accustomed to doing, things like making money. The television popped on and the CBS News anchor sat in the middle of the screen watching him. He didn't move, he didn't say anything. He didn't do anything other than watch him, then he smiled.

"They're coming for you," he said.

Mob closed his eyes telling himself that none of this was real. After a few concentrated efforts, he began to feel at peace again. He opened his eyes to see that the television was now off. He slowly began to get up, but his senses warned him to be still. He spotted something out the corner of his eye, there underneath his bed. Whatever it was, it wasn't supposed to be there. He'd been haunted by her presence for well over the past year.

"This isn't real. This isn't real. This isn't real!" Mob stopped himself from getting up afraid of what any sudden movement might provoke. He slowly slid back across the floor until his back hit the wall. The woman slithered from beneath the bed, bones popping, pale flesh. Her utter nakedness was a horrific sight in itself. Mob closed his eyes once again trying to make himself believe it was all in his head.

"It's not real. It's not real. It's not real!" He could smell her now. The stench reeking from her body was so strong that he had to open his eyes.

"I am real!" She lunged for his face, taking hold of it both hands. She covered his mouth with her own and tried to force her tongue into it.

"*Mhhhhh! Smmhhhh! Mhhhhhhh!*" Mob fought for dear life to break free.

He could feel her tongue prying at his lips to try and slip inside. He dug his fingers into her face, clawing at it, ripping her flesh apart. He could feel her cold hard tongue in his mouth now, slipping deeper and deeper down his throat.

He gagged.

Mob awoke, nearly choking as vomit threatened to erupt from inside. If the horrific nightmares didn't stop soon, he'd promised himself in that very moment that he'd seek help. His cell phone rang next to him on the nightstand. Any other time he'd be reluctant to accept the call, but after all that he'd just been through, he needed to hear someone's voice.

"What it do, fam-o?" It was Young Syke. Mob gratefully sat up in bed dabbing at his mouth with the sheets. "I hope you wasn't still sleep cause I got some fucked up shit to tell you."

"I'm awake, dawg," Mob replied. "But I just had another crazy-ass muthafuckin' dream. That shit is startin' to feel more and more real to me. Like a nigga can't wake up. I'm beginning to think that I might need some help."

Instead of Syke inquiring about what he'd dreamed, he went on to tell him about everything that had happened. Instantly, Mob started to wonder was Plocko behind the hit. Being that he'd just killed his second in command, Mob needed to be certain that the hit wasn't retaliation.

"Have everyone down at the shop in exactly one hour," Mob spoke sternly. "I'll need to know a play by play of everything that happened. Because, if Plocko had anything to do with this shit, then we'd best get ready."

***

Early that morning, Plocko sat in his bedroom staring at the television. His attention wandered somewhere in between his emotional state, his hate, betrayal, revenge, and finally confused. Who would dare kill someone that worked for him? That question alone had baffled him because whoever did it knew that he'd retaliate.

Thoughts of April settled back at the center of his attention. It had been a week and a day since she'd left. He'd been led to believe that she was only accompanying her friends back home. Strangely enough, it had also been one week and a day since Juan was murdered. His death left Plocko trying to connect the dots between April's absence, and Juan's demise. He questioned everything he knew about April. But no matter how hard he tried to convince himself that she was just young and living life to the fullest, the rumors forced him to accept another harsh reality.

Shortly after April disappeared, Plocko had several of his men try and track her down. Finding her would prove to be no problem. The cars that she drove were all owned by him. Although nothing was ever exposed as to who she was away visiting, Plocko now knew where she was staying. It was only a matter of time before everything else he'd wanted to know would be revealed.

Plocko ordered his new second in command to find out as much as he could about Slim's case. What he'd found out was that Slim had just hired David Longborrow.

Plocko was pleased to know that Slim had acquired such good representation. Although his new attorney wouldn't disclose specifics in regards to Slim's case, he did relay a message to him that his very close associates were inquiring about his case. David Longborrow gave Slim, Luis' number, and the rest was history. Slim was finally back connected with the Cartel, now he could get down to business.

Slim informed Luis of everything that was going on with his case. He went on to tell him about Derrick and how Mob had failed to execute the Feds star witness. As far as he knew, only two confidential witnesses were taking the stand against him. One of which was Derrick Walker and the other was still a mystery. The District Attorney concealed the identity of the second person arguing that one of Slim's henchmen would try and kill them. Slim had no idea who the other person was. The only other person it could be, he'd left her dead on a barn floor. If it wasn't for the Feds raiding the spot when they had, Slim's vicious Rottweilers would have eaten the skin off of April's bones.

Lucky for him, he'd heard the vehicles swarm the property before they kicked the door in. Federal Agents found him shortly after hid out in the woods. The only thing that connected him to even being there, was April and his truck.

Slim went on to tell Luis about McCracken and Agent Stevens. He'd told them that they'd stop at nothing until they brought down their entire operation. Slim was very clear about making sure that those two Agents needed to disappear. If by chance they continued to dig into the Crimson Mafia's business, it would only be a matter of time before they came looking for Plocko.

A gentle tap at his bedroom door brought Plocko out of his thoughts. "Come in!" he barked.

Maria sauntered into his room carrying a small tray of breakfast. "Be careful with this food, senor. I just finished making it, so everything is hot!"

Plocko eyed her curiously. He liked her, not only because of the sex but because he felt he could trust her. "Come sit," he insisted and patted the bed with his hand. He swung his feet out of bed so he could sit next to her. "There are some very troubling things happening in my organization. Things that tell me, someone that is close to me—is no good."

Maria nodded that she understood, yet, remained quiet. She knew all too well of the things that concerned Plocko. Although she was only but a servant to him, she was paid to be everything April was not.

"I truly don't know what to do about this situation," Plocko continued. "The person that has me so distraught is someone that means a lot to me."

Maria allowed a moment of silence, out of respect for his feelings. She sensed how terribly worried he was, simply by the manner in which he spoke. "Go with your heart," she finally replied. "I don't say that for my own benefit, I say that for you! If you have doubts about someone you're dealing with, then leave them alone. There are plenty of people willing to take their place. You don't need no one around that you can't trust."

Plocko smiled and patted her leg. It was because of conversations like these that made him value their relationship more. After all the time that he'd known her, he figured it was time to put her to the test.

"From now on, you no longer work for me," he said.

Maria looked shocked. "But senor—I didn't mean to offend you. I thought you wanted to know my opinion about what was troubling you?"

Plocko held up his hand to silence her. "Why do you think I need someone like you to work for me?"

Maria thought about it but couldn't respond. She'd done everything he'd ever asked of her, for him to want to fire her had her baffled. "Because I'm loyal and I'll do anything for you," she finally replied. "Whatever you want me to do, I'll do it."

Plocko shook his head in disgust everyone that worked for him would pledge such loyalty to him. The real question was, did she mean it.

"You say that you'll do anything for me, but are just talking, or do you mean it? If I were to ask you to kill for me, would you do it?"

Maria's mind was reeling, she wasn't a killer by far, nor had she so much as harmed another person, As much as she'd liked to say that was something she would do, she couldn't.

"I guess I must've been right," he stated confidently. "Your words are filled with empty promises and that is why you must leave!"

Maria glared at him with a look laced with contempt. Why he thought that she'd just walk away so easily, was beyond her understanding. "If you want me to kill then that's what I'll do. But for the record— I'm not going anywhere!"

Plocko glared at her with the same intensity that she looked upon him with. He expected her to cower away, but she appeared defiant.

"See, this is why you can no longer work for me," he said while laughing softly. "I can always count on you no matter what. Unlike April—" his voice trailed off into silence as ill thoughts resurfaced in his mind. Why wasn't she there to comfort his conflicting thoughts? He loved her with all his heart. He thought surely she felt the same way. He'd have done anything for April including kill one of his most loyal associates, but all that had suddenly changed.

"Do you want me to kill her?" Maria asked, noting the troubled expression etched on Plocko's face. But that was a statement that was easier said than done. April wasn't some random woman he'd fell in love with. She'd been groomed for men like him. Killing her would be no easy task.

"What makes you think that she'll let you just walk up to her and kill her?"

Maria shrugged. "There's a million ways to get rid of that problem. If you want me to do it, then I will."

Plocko leaned back on his pillows pondering his next move. Maria killing April wasn't even an option he'd actually entertained happening. He had professional hitmen to handle things like that. For now, his main objective was to find out if April was working with the Feds.

"If ever I decide for you to do it, I'll let you know," he spoke seriously. "For now, it's okay to carry on like you do whenever she is not around. We no longer have to hide anything from her. I am the boss. If she has a problem with the way that I do things—" he smirked. "I'll kill her myself."

Maria placed her hand on his thigh and slid it inside his robe. "If I am no longer a servant for you, she is going to be very upset about this."

Plocko yanked at the strap on his robe opening it so that she could take hold of what she'd been searching for. "Who cares if she is angry. Let me worry about her. All I need you to focus on is this sleeping monster that you've just woke up."

Chapter 18

Unexpected Visit

"Good morning!" Cynthia announced walking straight into Derrick's office, sitting down in front of his desk. "You'll have to excuse me for being so rude and not knocking, but I'm excited to hear what you did over the weekend."

Derrick was pouring himself a cup of coffee when she walked in. When he heard her voice, he couldn't do anything but laugh. "I guess this is what it feels like to be served with a no-knock search warrant? You're just gonna roll up in my office and demand that I start telling you my business?"

"Maybe you shouldn't be so dramatic. Now, if I had handcuffs you might have a valid point. But seeing as though I don't—I'm listening." Derrick laughed out loud as he set the coffee pot back down and went to take his seat.

That was the first time Cynthia had seen him up close since he'd returned. She instantly noticed the large diamond earrings, diamond-studded watch, and bracelet. "Well, don't you look nice? Did a weekend getaway cause you to splurge on yourself like this? Or did you meet someone new?"

"Dig-dig-dig. You really have no limits, do you? First, you walk into my office without knocking—"

"But I apologized for that."

"Then you sat down without being offered to."

"Would you like for me to stand?"

"Now you wanna know if I met someone new?" Derrick hit a few buttons on his computer trying to busy himself to avoid any more questions.

"I called you several times," Cynthia went on to say. "I guess you were either too busy, or you were just trying to avoid my calls."

"Dig-dig-dig. You can ask as many questions as you'd like, but I'm not telling." To let the truth be told, Derrick had seen Cynthia calling him throughout the weekend. He didn't answer the phone because he couldn't risk someone knowing that he still had dealings with April. "I saw that you called, but I was out of town on vacation. A vacation means, I'm taking a break from things. Whether that be work, the phone, people that want to ask me a million questions, if you can think of it—that's what I was taking a break from."

Cynthia shot him a look that could kill, and said, "I see someone is back in their shell again."

"See, there you go with the extras. I already told you how bad I've been needing to take that vacation. If you think about everything that happened last year, you'd—" Derrick was kicking himself in the ass no soon as he realized what he'd just said. He was almost certain that Cynthia would inquire about what had happened, but amazingly, she didn't.

"Hopefully, you had a great time," she went on to say. "And now that you're back hopefully we'll get back on our workout schedule."

Derrick peered over at her as she gave him a strange look. It wasn't a look that said she was waiting for confirmation. It was a look that said, *I know what you did, and it better not happen again!*

"Why wouldn't we get back to our normal routine? That's a no brainer. As a matter of fact—" A gentle knock at his office door drew his attention.

"I hope I'm not interrupting anything," April said as she entered the room. "I just stopped by to let you know that I was back in town. Plus, I haven't set foot in this place in like forever!"

Derrick peered up at her in utter disbelief. *How could she be so bold as to show up there?*

"What a surprise to see you again!" Cynthia exclaimed, filing an uncomfortable moment of silence. "How have you been? You look great. I was starting to think that I'd never see you again."

April looked at Cynthia as if she was the scum of the earth.

"And you are?"

Cynthia looked surprised that she had forgotten who she was. "It's me—Cynthia. I got hired here shortly after you took your first leave of absence. I had the chance to work with you for a while when you came back, though."

April pondered her what she'd said for a moment, then casually strolled around Derrick's desk. "Can't say that I remember you," she replied. "Sorry."

April went on to look at Derrick who still had a bewildered expression on his face. "And how are you doing this morning? I hope I didn't freak you out by showing up here?"

Derrick quickly stood up and gave her a hug. "Oh, no-no-no, I'm good. You might've thrown me off for a second, but I'm fine." He suddenly cleared his throat, instantly coming up with a plan to get out of the limelight. "I thought surely you'd remember working with Cynthia. She's always been one of my better employees. But seeing as though you don't, Cynthia, this is April. April, this is Cynthia, my new unofficial slash official, store manager."

April peered over at Cynthia expressing obvious contempt and said, "We've met. Once again, I'm here because we need to talk."

Derrick instantly picked up on the ice in her tone. "Cynthia, if you don't mind, I'd like to have a word with April for a moment."

Cynthia nodded, stood, and gave both of them a warm smile before excusing herself.

"Oh, and Cynthia," April said, stopping her before she left the room. "If you'll be so kind as to close the door behind you. Derrick and I will be needing a little privacy." April forced a weak smile to convey the message that Cynthia's presence was no longer welcomed.

"Do you mind telling me, what the hell that was about?" Derrick snapped, coming to Cynthia's defense after she left his office. "She was just being polite and the best thing you could think to do was be rude."

April stepped closer to him and pulled him towards her by his shirt. "I just needed to be clear that this—" She gently shoved him away and walked back around to take the seat Cynthia had been sitting in. "—is off-limits."

Derrick scoffed. "And just what in the hell is that supposed to mean?"

"It means exactly what you think I mean. If I have to risk losing my life just to give you what you want—"

"I didn't ask you to do anything."

"And I didn't say that you did. But, if I'm going to risk giving up everything including my life, it's only right that you give up something as well."

Derrick laughed and said, "So, you're blackmailing me?"

April crossed her legs and peered up at him with a devilish smirk. Regardless of what he thought about her, she'd stop at nothing until she had what she wanted. "I'm sure I made myself perfectly clear about the way I feel about you. Do you think I would've invested so much time, and hard-earned money if I'd have felt otherwise?"

Derrick leaned on his desk and looked her dead in the eye. "You-can't—buy me, April."

"Who said I was trying too? I did what I did because I wanted to, not because I expected something out of it. But you can rest assured—there are plenty of people that would appreciate a woman like me on their arm. I guess that would mean, the only thing I need to be careful about wasting too much of, is my time." She stood to leave feeling that her presence was unwelcome.

"April, wait," Derrick said. He couldn't afford to let her leave. To let her walk away now would put him right back at square one. "It's going to take some time for me to adjust to you. You can't expect me to just up and forget everything that's happened."

"I don't expect you to, but the blame doesn't just lie on me, it lies with you, too! You made that choice to step out on your wife, not me."

164

"Easssyyyy, now."

April smacked her lips and continued to press on, "Maybe if you would've told me the truth from the very start, none of this would've happened."

Derrick stormed around his desk and marched right up to her face. "You need to be careful about what comes out of your mouth," he spat.

"If the shoe fits, wear it."

"April."

"It's tha truth!"

"Aprillll!"

She gave him a distasteful once over and said, "I'm not afraid of you, Derrick. Your threats don't scare me. Instead of trying to put fear in someone that fears no man, maybe you should be concerned with what brought me here in the first place."

A look of curiosity flickered across his face. Now instead of standing there mugging her, Derrick's facial expression had softened. "Why did you come here?"

April laughed and turned to leave. "Wouldn't you like to know?" she replied sarcastically. "I'll give you some time to figure things out. And when you make up your mind about what you're willing to give up, give me a call."

***

Later That Night

It was well past 9 P.M. by the time Derrick made it home for the evening. His usual workout with Cynthia had turned into a full-blown argument. Cynthia was furious about April's sarcastic remarks and felt that Derrick should've corrected her on the spot.

Derrick couldn't believe how jealous Cynthia had become over the brief exchange between him and April. No matter how hard he stressed that they were only friends, Cynthia insisted that it was much more than that. This was exactly why he hated to mix business with personal relationships. Although Cynthia and Derrick had never spoken one word about being involved in a relationship, they'd still managed to feel strangely committed.

Derrick strolled into his living room and sat down on the sofa. It had been a long mentally draining day. Now that he'd taken a hot shower it was time to relax, to some smooth R&B. *Forever I'm Ready* by *Jeremih*, filled the living room with soulful sounds. Derrick couldn't do anything but shake his head at the thoughts dancing around in his head about Cynthia. She was cool. Someone he could talk to. Someone he could chill with. Regardless of whatever road their relationship had taken a turn down, he valued their friendship above all.

Thoughts of April soon began to resurface in his mind. He thought back to how their relationship began, which was a lot like his and Cynthia's. He cursed himself for allowing himself to bring yet another person into such a deadly situation. Anyone close to him stood the chance of losing their life.

Memories of his wife and son soon began to settle back into his thoughts. Not only had he not been to see them, but he'd allowed the thoughts of them to become occupied by someone else. Not even two weeks ago he was prowling the streets looking for the people that had murdered his family. Now, here he was dwelling on relationships that he had with other women. Derrick felt like shit.

But he was starting to understand what was going on inside him. When his wife and son were brutally killed, that left a void. Not only was he unable to be happy with himself, but he was unable to be happy with others, as well. But when he allowed Cynthia into just a tiny space in his life, she brought happiness in with her. Feelings that he'd long since forgotten, had slowly come back to memory.

The strange feeling of commitment he felt towards Cynthia was only because of the gratitude he had towards her. She'd begun to fill the void. Teaching him to stand tall, whereas before he was crippled. Teaching him to breathe when he was slowly suffocating.

A smile began to form on Derrick's face, he was thankful to feel alive again. Instead of continuing to chase happiness away, he'd made up his mind to let happiness in. The first thing the next morning, he'd stop by and have a much-needed talk with his wife. A piece of his heart would always belong to her, but he could no longer carry the guilt that he felt.

Adrian Dulan

Chapter 19

The Plot Thickens

The next morning, Derrick awoke to the sound of his alarm clock blaring in his ear. Instead of getting up and getting dressed for work he threw on something a little more comfortable. While standing in his full-length mirror he began to second guess his intentions. Was he really ready to do what he was about to do? Was happiness really worth what he was about to give up?

Derrick released a loud frustrating sigh and ran his hands over his face. There was no question whether his happiness was worth what he was about to give up. It was because of his fear of letting go that made him have doubts.

Derrick snatched his gun off the dresser and stood peering down at it. He'd bought it for a reason. He'd promised to kill everyone that had anything to do with killing his family. Yet, one year later not one person lied dead because of him. Was he serious about revenge, or had he only been misleading himself? He tucked his gun in the lining of his jeans, then threw on a black leather jacket. As long as he went through with what April offered him, the promise that he'd made to his wife would be fulfilled.

One hour later, Derrick drove through the gates at the cemetery. His wife's favorite song, *Angel* by *Bobby Valentino* hummed softly through his subs. Not so much as one person could be seen as he drove past row after row of graves. He was starting to feel as if that day had been ordained for him to do what he was there to do.

Derrick pulled alongside the grave he was there to visit and parked. As he stepped from his car, each step had suddenly become that much harder to take. He'd started having second thoughts about whether he could say what needed to be said. It was one thing to be at home and have the courage to say everything while looking in the bathroom mirror. But it took a lot more courage to say it while staring down at two headstones there because of your own mistakes.

Tears rolled down his cheeks as he fell to his knees and began to weep. "I'm sorry," he cried. "I never meant for any of this to happen. I was so caught up in my own stuff, that I didn't see all of this happening." He leaned over and kissed the headstones. He figured, if he laid all his guilt to rest, he might just have a chance at having a normal life again.

Derrick dug into his pocket and removed a small black box. Upon opening it, his thoughts reverted to the day that his wife slid the ring on his finger. They'd vowed to grow old together. They thought that they'd die together. They used to laugh about how things would be in the future. How it would feel to raise a family. How it would feel to have a family.

Derrick felt his temper rise at the thought of what he'd deprived his family of. "I didn't deserve you," he said solemnly and pulled the ring from the box. "I didn't deserve either of you. If I would've known that all this was going to happen, I would've done this a long time ago." He placed the ring on top of Martina's headstone and kissed it one last time. A wave of mixed emotions threatened to overcome him, but he held true to his word. There would be no more tears of guilt or sleepless nights. From that day on it was time for him to stand tall.

Derrick stood and peered into the light blue sky. He wondered if there was a heaven would his wife and son be looking down at him. He wondered would they forgive him for what he'd done, and would he ever see them again.

Suddenly, he began to feel stupid for ever having allowed himself to wonder such things. If there was a heaven, then there most certainly was a hell. But if there was a God where was he when he'd asked for his help? Where was God when those people came into his home and murdered his whole family?

Derrick cursed himself for ever having said that prayer the night that his family was killed. He'd put his faith in the unseen only to find out how alone he actually was. Derrick walked back to his car and was just about to get in when a strong gust of wind blew. He stumbled back, shielding his eyes from the blinding dirt.

A cold chill ran up his spine as the wind began to howl. His eyes popped open when a strange feeling as if he were being watched came over him. He spun around scanning everything within sight. He saw nothing but headstones for as far as the eye could see. Just as the idea came across his mind that he might be tripping, the wind blew again. Dead leaves skipped across the grass as the trees swayed in the distance. It was so quiet that he could hear a pin drop. Derrick wiped at his irritated eyes still stinging from the dust, then he heard it.

"I've always been here."

Instantly, Derrick went for his gun and aimed it into the wind. He peered down inside his car, over the top of it, around it, beside it. Nothing! He'd heard that voice the night his son was murdered. He'd prayed for strength, strength to burst from the closet and save his only child, and that's when he heard it.

"Be still."

Derrick fumbled with the door latch and quickly slid inside. He'd yet to start the car before he noticed it. Everything was surprisingly still, a frozen moment in time. The trees no longer swayed in the distance. The leaves no longer skipped across the lawn. Still. Quiet. At peace. The sudden calmness was so utterly staggering, Derrick had to force himself to start his car and drive away. The further away from the grave that he drove, the more he began to feel like his old self again. He could only assume that what he'd felt was the beginning stages of a mental break down. His assumptions only made him that much more determined to do what he was there to do.

There was one more stop he had to make before his mission at the cemetery was complete. His son's biological mother, Erica was buried in the same cemetery. He had a few choice words that he needed to say to her as well.

Derrick drove for yet a little while longer, making a few turns here and there, until he finally ended up where he needed to be. It had been a while since he'd visited Erica. She too stirred up mixed emotions because his actions had cost her life as well. Derrick cut off his car and quickly got out. As he drew near to Erica's grave, he noticed an older black man propped up against Erica's headstone. He carelessly guzzled down a bottle of Wild Irish Rose, while fluid dripped from the corners of his mouth. His clothing was very much outdated. He wore a shaggy long beard that was mostly white, and his hair was filthy and matted.

"What up, bruh?" Derrick greeted him as he walked up. He noted how badly malnourished the man looked. He looked like he was strung out on drugs, or something worse like he was dying. "Are you all right over here? Do you need me to call you some help?"

The man's head snapped back, accidentally bumping into Erica's headstone. "Bruh?" he slurred, revealing a mouth full of heavily stained teeth. "Did you hear this muthafucka?" he asked peering down at Erica's grave. "He says, am— I— good?"

Derrick smirked, choosing to hold his tongue to avoid a confrontation. "Look, I hate to break up your little party, but I came here to spend some time with my kid's mother. I think you may have made a mistake and ended up at the wrong place. This here belongs to someone that was very close to me."

The man bolted up straight, his head bobbing up and down as if he couldn't control it. He peered down at Erica's grave, then back up at Derrick. "*Made a mistake?* Nigga, you the one that made a mistake!"

Derrick gritted on the man, quickly growing frustrated. "This ain't what you want," he warned him. "Either you can find some other place to hang out, or I'ma find someplace for you."

The older man bated his grill and spat, "I don't take to kindly to threats, nigga. If you think you can whoop me, then gon' and do it." He slowly rose to his feet, staggered two steps forward, then two steps back. He picked up his bottle and swiped at the grass clinging to it. "Do you know who tha' fuck

I am?"

Derrick looked at him like he was crazy and said, "I don't give a damn who you are. I didn't come here to argue with a drunk. I came here to visit with her." He pointed at Erica's headstone hoping that the man would catch his drift.

"Well, I'll be damned." The man held up his bottle to the sun inspecting it, then guzzled down the last of it. He stood swaying for a moment, then looked at his bottle, lifted it, saw a little liquid still left in the corner, then drank that too! "You can't be here to see her," he began, "I'm here to see her!" He cocked back to throw the bottle at Derrick, but it slipped out of his hand behind him. "It's because of you that she left me in the first place. If-if-if—" He doubled over and began coughing, spit dangled from his lips prompting him to wipe it away with his sleeve. "All this happened because of you!" The man yelled. "If Erica hadn't ever met your punk ass, she'd still be alive."

Derrick's heart felt like it had skipped a beat. He couldn't believe what he'd just heard. How did the man know about Erica? Did he know about what happened? Did he know about his son? Suddenly Derrick had a million things that he wanted to ask the man, but ultimately, he decided to simply let it go. "I think you just drunk and rambling off the first thang that comes to mind," Derrick replied, convincing himself of the matter more so than the person he was talking to.

"Who just rambling thangs off?"

"You."

"How you gon' tell me what I'm doin? I know Erica, I used to be with Erica."

Derrick forcefully laughed. "Whatever ol' school. Now you startin' to sound like the clown that you look like."

"*Clown?* Yo' momma looks like a clown, nigga. You must don't know who you're fuckin' wit'?"

Derrick shook his head and said, "I don't."

The man laughed as if he knew the biggest best-kept secret. "Well, I'm-not gon' tell you, either. You just keep right on switchin' yo' happy ass around and carryin' on like you all that. You doing all that fakin' like you my son's daddy, but you ain't shit!"

Derrick squinted. "What did you just say to me?"

"I said, you—ain't my son's daddy. Do you want me to spell it out for you? Capital Y—O—U. A—I—N comma T. S—H—I—T! How's that?"

Derrick slowly drew closer now sizing the man up. "Rewind that shit to when you said that I'm playing daddy."

The man chuckled some more. "I said it, and I meant it! You wanna be me, I'm sure she told you that can't nobody make it thunderclap like I did. Erica loved me. She was only with you because you was convenient. If I wasn't gettin' high, ain't no way she woulda named my son after you."

Derrick's knees buckled. He clearly remembered his wife's voice telling him that Jr. wasn't his. She always had doubts, but he didn't listen. Thoughts from the day his son was born flashed vividly across his mind. The baby looked just like his mother, he had the same eyes as her, the same nose, but why was Erica crying? Why was she crying when he'd asked to hold his son? Did she feel guilty about something? Did she know something, he didn't?

Derrick glared down at the sickly-looking man that now stood chest to chest with him. But unbeknown to him, he'd finally reached his breaking point. What he did next would come back to haunt him for years to come.

***

"Today is my anniversary," Stevens exclaimed as McCracken clicked away on his computer. "I plan to go home and eat a good home-cooked meal. Then, we may even catch up on some of our favorite shows. I might even take a little time to listen to Margaret read from one of her new novels."

McCracken shook his head while looking upon him in utter disbelief. "That really sounds boring, you know? You should take Margaret out to a nice dinner, or even buy her a ring or something."

Stevens waved his statement off and replied, "We've been there and done that. Margaret isn't hard to please when it comes to anniversaries and holidays. I don't have to fly her out to Paris or some extravagant resort. Our love doesn't require us to spend thousands on each other."

McCracken nodded in understanding. Stevens had been with his wife for more than thirty years. If anyone knew what she liked, it would be him.

"Have you heard anything from Brown, yet?" McCracken asked, quickly changing the subject, he then picked up the newspaper and settled back in his chair.

"Not lately, I've called him several times. I even had one of the guys stop by to check on him. They said it looked like he hadn't been home in a few days. The mail was piled up in the mailbox, and Foxy was barking so much that they went around back to find, she hadn't had any food or water in her dish."

McCracken sat silently pondering everything that could possibly be going on. Agent Brown knew that they were about to start serving indictments, so his sudden disappearance did seem rather strange. "Let's not jump to far ahead of ourselves," he began, "I understand what you're telling me does sound a little odd, but he's an undercover Agent. Let's just wait a while before we start jumping to any conclusions. That'll give him a chance to report in and then this whole mess will be over."

Stevens smiled. "That sounds like music to my ears. Once this case is over, I plan to retire. I told Margaret we would go anywhere she wanted, and I plan to hold true to my word."

McCracken smiled as well he too was at the point of retiring. It was because of this case that they'd been working that he still had yet to follow through with it. "Did you get a chance to check out this paper?" McCracken asked while peering down at it curiously. "Says here, an entire family was gunned down inside of their apartment in the Hill Side Courtz.

Two officers were also killed while trying to apprehend the suspects. Police were unable to find the people that were responsible for doing it." McCracken peered across the desk at Stevens expecting some sort of explanation. "Isn't that the same area we're about to start serving warrants?"

"Sure is. That's why I was giving you that look when I told you about Brown. He's been missing since the night all of that happened. So, now do you think we should try and contact him a little sooner than later?"

McCracken's eyebrows arched. "Nah, I think we should stick with the plan. I believe Brown knows what he's doing. He's a quick thinker. I'm confident he'll find a way to let us know if something has gone wrong."

Stevens' phone rang interrupting their conversation. "This is Stevens," he answered the call. He sat listening as someone spoke on the other end. Whatever was being said had to be important because he was already out of his chair sliding on his coat. "Don't do a thing until we get there!" he barked and slammed the phone down.

McCracken peered up at him quizzically and asked, "What was all that about?"

"That was the District Attorney. He says that Derrick almost killed a man in the cemetery today."

"He did what! That's our star witness."

My point exactly. The D.A said that whoever the guy was had two small packets of a powdery substance in his pocket. It tested positive to be Heroin. The state isn't going to do any paperwork on Derrick because of us. But we need to get over there and find out what in the hell just happened."

***

Margaret rushed inside her home carrying several bags from the grocery store. She hated that it was cold outside. Had it not been for her anniversary being that day, she'd have gladly waited until it was much warmer before going out. Margaret had been up since eight that morning trying to prepare for that night. She planned to have a candlelight dinner, cozy up in front of the fireplace, and do whatever else that came to mind.

Upon walking into the kitchen, she felt a cold draft blow in through the back door. She quickly sat the bags on the counter and went to check out the source of the problem. The back door stood ajar, which instantly heightened her suspicion. She carefully examined the door checking to make sure it wasn't open because of forced entry. After a brief inspection, she concluded that there'd been no break-in. Stevens had taught her a lot during his stint as a DEA Agent. He'd taught her how to protect herself and how to detect danger when she couldn't see it.

Margaret stood still listening to the sounds of her home. She'd been in that old house for well over twenty years. She could stand in the middle of the kitchen blindfolded and still know which door you opened just by the sound of the hinges creaking. She listened intently as the soft rustle of leaves blew outside in the cool breeze. She could hear the neighbor's dog barking in the distance but heard nothing that sounded out of place. Finally, feeling as if she were safe, she closed the door and made a mental note to tell her husband when he'd returned.

Margaret made her way back into the kitchen and quickly started putting groceries away. Just as she opened the refrigerator a creepy feeling that she was being watched, came over her. She scanned the dining room to the living room, laundry room, and finally the back door. As much as she'd like to believe that it was all in her head, it wasn't.

Margaret calmly closed the refrigerator back acting as if she suspected nothing. Her gut warned her that she needed to get out of there as quickly as possible. She walked back through the dining room to the living room and opened the front door, that's when she heard the closet open behind her.

"Going somewhere?" a man snarled.

Margaret spun around trembling and said, "What are you doing in here?"

The intruder calmly strolled toward her while keeping his gun pointed at her head. "I'm here to see you," he replied. "Stevens not here, no? I will only be here for a second, yes. I was told to deliver him a message."

Tears began ho roll down Margaret's cheek. She could only assume that this had something to do with the case Stevens had been working on. "My husband is not here," she stated firmly. "You can take whatever money I have and go. I won't tell anyone that you came here."

The man chuckled as he slowly inched toward her and said, "Oh, I plan to. That's part of the message I'll be leaving for your husband."

Chapter 20

The Beginning of The End

Mob sped through the city streets on a mission. His mind raced to piece the puzzle together concerning the uncertain future of the Crimson Mafia. Not only did they lose a major cash cow by losing the Hill Side Courtz, but they were still in the blind about who was behind the hit. In addition to everything that had been going on, there was still the situation with 4 Lyfe. Did he have something to do with the hit? Why did he leave his post? Young Syke was almost certain that he had something to do with it. After he'd closed down shop that night, he had Baby Jerk and Block Monsta to take him for a ride. Had it not been for Mob's orders, he'd be dead. Only time would tell if he made the right choice by keeping him alive.

"Yo, Syke!" Mob called out as he walked into his condo. "You ready to go, yet?" Mob walked into the living room and sat down on the sofa. Spotting a partially smoked blunt in the ashtray, he picked it up and lit it.

"I'll be down in a second, fam-o. Give me 'bout ten, and I'll be ready."

Mob scooped up the remote and hit the power. *Loaded Bases* by *Nipsey Hussle* bang through his house speakers. Mob hit the blunt and began thinking about their up and coming meeting with the Steady Grinding Boyz. He'd made up his mind that if they started acting nervous, then they must've been in on the hit. The only reason he'd decided to let 4 Lyfe live was to keep the tension down. They already had enough stacked against them. They were in dire need of more soldiers.

Syke nudged him on the arm while peering down at him with genuine concern. "Damn, fam-o. You didn't hear me calling your name all them times?"

Mob glared up at him, surprised that he was suddenly there. What had felt like a mere couple of minutes was more like a half-hour. "My bad, I ain't heard shit," Mob stated as a matter-of-factly. "A nigga zoned out thinkin' 'bout all this shit we up against. I guess it don't help none that I'm in here smokin' on this gas." He lifted what he thought to be a blunt only to find all that remained was ashes.

"You a'ight, fam-o? You sure you ready to have this meeting with these fools?"

Mob started to explain but quickly decided against it. "I'm good, damu. Let's head over to the spot cause I'm a little anxious to get to the bottom of some things."

The entire ride over to the meeting place, Syke sat studying Mob closely. Everything about him had changed. He was there, but his mind was always elsewhere. Whenever Syke looked him in the eye, he didn't see the same boss that he'd come to know through the years. He saw a ticking time bomb that was ready to destroy everything at the drop of a dime.

"Do you know whose truck that is?" Mob asked as he drove into the parking lot of an abandoned warehouse that they used for secret meetings.

Young Syke quickly gathered his thoughts. "Ain't that the same truck that them niggaz rolled up in last time?"

Mob didn't respond. He continued to eye the truck suspiciously as they pulled up and parked. The last time Lil Menace showed up in the same SUV, didn't mean anything. But now that Mob had seen two DEA Agents get out of the same kind of truck, he had to be cautious with what he was doing whenever he saw one around.

Both Mob and Young Syke got out and greeted the other two Goon Squad members already there waiting for them. 4 Lyfe was the only one that was nowhere in sight. After the way they punished him the other night, he couldn't walk or talk, even if he wanted to.

"What up, fam?" Mob greeted Lil Menace and Big Crip as they exited the white Durango.

No one appeared to be of good spirits. Everyone had a mug on their faces seemingly looking for any reason to turn this peaceful meeting into a blood bath.

"I don't know, my nigga," Lil Menace answered. "I see you brought them Goonies with you again?"

Mob smirked, picking up on his sarcasm. "How 'bout you and I take a little walk?" he said. "I have a small business proposition that I'd like to offer you. We can leave everyone else over here to get more familiar. How's that sound?"

Lil Menace cut his eyes over at Big Crip, then glared at Young Syke. "That shit sounds good than a muthafucka," he snarled. "I'm so sick of lookin' at this fake ass nigga already."

Mob glared at him momentarily. Lil Menace literally didn't care about their agreement they made before. Being that there were so many serious issues that needed to be discussed, Mob chalked it up as a sign that the Steady Grinding Boyz didn't have anything to do with the hit.

"As you know, we've been connected with a serious plug for quite some time?" Mob began, "And, sometimes, good business relationships come to an end. The people we're connected to, no doubt have been good to us. But—" Movement out the corner of his eye had suddenly distracted him.

Big Crip opened the back door of the SUV and said something to the driver. From that point on, he had to know whose truck that was.

"Who's driving that Durango?" Mob asked.

Lil Menace narrowed his eyes trying to get a better read on where that question had come from. "Nigga, fuck that truck. What you was sayin' about your plug?"

Mob ice grilled him to the point that both men stood staring at each other. It was perfectly clear that Lil Menace had no idea who he was dealing with. "If you wanna talk about my connect, we'll do that after I find out who's in that truck."

Lil Menace looked back over his shoulder. Playing little man to people that he absolutely hated was proving to be more of a challenge then it was worth. "Hey, cuz, tell Bang to step out the truck for a minute!" Lil Menace hollered out to Big Crip. "This nigga Mob tryin' to see who tha fuck drivin'."

Mob looked on curiously, taking a few steps closer. As soon as the front door came open, he instantly recognized the driver. "Nigga, that's the Feds!" he hissed and spun around to look Menace in the eye. "You niggaz tryin' to get us knocked?"

Lil Menace looked confused. He had no idea what Mob was talking about. Although something about Bang wasn't adding up, he clearly recalled what they'd done the other night. Luckily, Crazy Cuz suggested that they keep Bang close after they'd got away. They couldn't afford to let him go home and accidentally tell his girl what they'd done. "Is you sure that cuz is one-time?"

"I'm positive that nigga is tha jakes! Y'all can roll tha dice and continue to fuck with him if you want to. But me and my niggaz is out."

Lil Menace stood watching as Mob shuffled over to his car. As much as he hated to admit it, he was starting to believe that Mob was right.

***

Agent Stevens slid his key into the door and quickly unlocked it. He was glad to finally be home. Glad to be away from the constant hustle and bustle that his job consisted of. Glad to finally be in a position to where he could finally relax.

"Margaret, I'm home!" Stevens walked through the front door expecting to smell the sweet aroma of a good home-cooked meal. Instead, the unsettling darkness had set him on alarm. He cautiously walked into the living room and clicked on the lamp. He called out his wife's name once again but was met by more silence. Margaret was always sitting right there in the living room when he came in from work. For the house to be so dark, with an eerie feeling flooding his senses, Stevens quickly began to suspect foul play and drew his weapon.

Tiptoeing toward the kitchen, Stevens listened intently for anything that may sound out of place. A soft ticking could be heard from a Grandfather clock in the far corner of the room.

Windowpanes rattled from the howling winds demanding to be allowed inside. The feverish thump of his heartbeat beating in his chest. Stevens held his breath gripping ever so tightly on his gun. He peeked around the corner into the kitchen. He thought he saw something, but it was dark. He spun into the kitchen leading with his gun. His eyes danced wildly around in the darkness. He flipped on the light, several bags of groceries were still sitting on the counter. Stevens spared a peek inside one of the bags. The food had thawed, Margaret's purse sat alongside the bags on the counter.

She's got to be home, he thought. *But why would she leave all this food out?*

Stevens made his way down the hall, checking the laundry room and the downstairs bathroom. Nothing. He peered upstairs; it was dark, darker than the darkness he'd encountered when he came inside. Stevens slowly climbed the stairs taking each step one at a time. Each step closer to the top he got, the louder each step creaked. Fear gripped his heart with a vicious hold, squeezing it until he felt that it would burst. He strained to see through the darkness that engulfed the second floor of his home, but that was impossible.

The darkness was impenetrable.

Stevens stopped in front of one of the kid's bedroom, listening for any sound. Although his kids had long since moved out, he still needed to be certain that he didn't hear anything. He crossed the hall to the next room and placed his ear to the door. Nothing. He placed his back against the wall and slid down the hall toward the master bedroom. It was deathly quiet, too quiet. He took a peek into the room. He couldn't see nothing but the red glow of numbers on the alarm clock.

Stevens cocked the hammer back on his gun. His gut warning him not to go any further. His heart rate raced out of control. He tried to focus in order to calm the ever-growing anxiety building in his chest. He reached out and hit the light switch.

"Noooooo!" Margaret laid face down with her hands tied behind her back. She was naked, blood could be seen smeared across her buttocks. The sheets had been stripped away, leaving her face down in a patch of dried blood. "Margaret," he cried. The smell of urine assaulted his nostrils. It was a distinctive smell that he never thought he'd smell in his very own home.

Stevens slowly crossed the room with his gun dangling along his side. He saw something long and pink, covered in blood, lying in the palm of her hand. he took another step closer; it was her tongue.

To Be Continued...
Glocks and Satin Sheets 3
Coming Soon

Submission Guideline

Submit the first three chapters of your completed manuscript to ldpsubmissions@gmail.com, subject line: Your book's title. The manuscript must be in a .doc file and sent as an attachment. Document should be in Times New Roman, double spaced and in size 12 font. Also, provide your synopsis and full contact information. If sending multiple submissions, they must each be in a separate email.

Have a story but no way to send it electronically? You can still submit to LDP/Ca$h Presents. Send in the first three chapters, written or typed, of your completed manuscript to:

LDP: Submissions Dept
Po Box 944
Stockbridge, Ga 30281

DO NOT send original manuscript. Must be a duplicate.

Provide your synopsis and a cover letter containing your full contact information.

Thanks for considering LDP and Ca$h Presents.

Adrian Dulan

Coming Soon from Lock Down Publications/Ca$h Presents

BOW DOWN TO MY GANGSTA

By **Ca$h**

TORN BETWEEN TWO

By **Coffee**

THE STREETS STAINED MY SOUL **II**

By **Marcellus Allen**

BLOOD OF A BOSS **VI**

SHADOWS OF THE GAME II

By **Askari**

LOYAL TO THE GAME **IV**

By **T.J. & Jelissa**

A DOPEBOY'S PRAYER **II**

By **Eddie "Wolf" Lee**

IF LOVING YOU IS WRONG... **III**

By **Jelissa**

TRUE SAVAGE **VII**

MIDNIGHT CARTEL III

DOPE BOY MAGIC IV

By **Chris Green**

BLAST FOR ME **III**

A SAVAGE DOPEBOY III

CUTTHROAT MAFIA II

By **Ghost**

A HUSTLER'S DECEIT III

KILL ZONE **II**

BAE BELONGS TO ME III

A DOPE BOY'S QUEEN II

By **Aryanna**

COKE KINGS V

KING OF THE TRAP II

By **T.J. Edwards**

GORILLAZ IN THE BAY V

De'Kari

THE STREETS ARE CALLING II

Duquie Wilson

KINGPIN KILLAZ IV

STREET KINGS III

PAID IN BLOOD III

CARTEL KILLAZ IV

DOPE GODS II

Hood Rich

SINS OF A HUSTLA II

ASAD

KINGZ OF THE GAME V

Playa Ray

SLAUGHTER GANG IV

RUTHLESS HEART IV

By Willie Slaughter

THE HEART OF A SAVAGE III

By Jibril Williams

FUK SHYT II

By Blakk Diamond

FEAR MY GANGSTA 5

THE REALEST KILLAS

By Tranay Adams

TRAP GOD II

By Troublesome

YAYO IV

Adrian Dulan

A SHOOTER'S AMBITION III
By S. Allen
GHOST MOB
Stilloan Robinson
KINGPIN DREAMS III
By Paper Boi Rari
CREAM
By Yolanda Moore
SON OF A DOPE FIEND II
By Renta
FOREVER GANGSTA II
GLOCKS ON SATIN SHEETS III
By Adrian Dulan
LOYALTY AIN'T PROMISED II
By Keith Williams
THE PRICE YOU PAY FOR LOVE II
DOPE GIRL MAGIC III
By Destiny Skai
CONFESSIONS OF A GANGSTA II
By Nicholas Lock
I'M NOTHING WITHOUT HIS LOVE II
By Monet Dragun
CAUGHT UP IN THE LIFE III
By Robert Baptiste
LIFE OF A SAVAGE IV
A GANGSTA'S QUR'AN II
By **Romell Tukes**
QUIET MONEY III
THUG LIFE II
By **Trai'Quan**

THE STREETS MADE ME III
By **Larry D. Wright**
THE ULTIMATE SACRIFICE VI
IF YOU CROSSM ME ONCE II
By **Anthony Fields**
THE LIFE OF A HOOD STAR
By **Ca$h & Rashia Wilson**

Available Now

RESTRAINING ORDER **I & II**
By **CA$H & Coffee**
LOVE KNOWS NO BOUNDARIES **I II & III**
By **Coffee**
RAISED AS A GOON I, II, III & IV
BRED BY THE SLUMS I, II, III
BLAST FOR ME I & II
ROTTEN TO THE CORE I II III
A BRONX TALE I, II, III
DUFFEL BAG CARTEL I II III IV
HEARTLESS GOON I II III IV
A SAVAGE DOPEBOY I II
HEARTLESS GOON I II III
DRUG LORDS I II III
CUTTHROAT MAFIA
By **Ghost**
LAY IT DOWN **I & II**
LAST OF A DYING BREED

Adrian Dulan

BLOOD STAINS OF A SHOTTA I & II III

By **Jamaica**

LOYAL TO THE GAME I II III

LIFE OF SIN I, II III

By **TJ & Jelissa**

BLOODY COMMAS I & II

SKI MASK CARTEL I II & III

KING OF NEW YORK I II,III IV V

RISE TO POWER I II III

COKE KINGS I II III IV

BORN HEARTLESS I II III IV

KING OF THE TRAP

By **T.J. Edwards**

IF LOVING HIM IS WRONG…I & II

LOVE ME EVEN WHEN IT HURTS I II III

By **Jelissa**

WHEN THE STREETS CLAP BACK I & II III

THE HEART OF A SAVAGE I II

By **Jibril Williams**

A DISTINGUISHED THUG STOLE MY HEART I II & III

LOVE SHOULDN'T HURT I II III IV

RENEGADE BOYS I II III IV

PAID IN KARMA I II III

By **Meesha**

A GANGSTER'S CODE I &, II III

A GANGSTER'S SYN I II III

THE SAVAGE LIFE I II III

CHAINED TO THE STREETS I II III

By **J-Blunt**

PUSH IT TO THE LIMIT

Glocks on Satin Sheets 2

By **Bre' Hayes**

BLOOD OF A BOSS **I, II, III, IV, V**

SHADOWS OF THE GAME

By **Askari**

THE STREETS BLEED MURDER **I, II & III**

THE HEART OF A GANGSTA I II& III

By **Jerry Jackson**

CUM FOR ME I II III IV V

An **LDP Erotica Collaboration**

BRIDE OF A HUSTLA **I II & II**

THE FETTI GIRLS **I, II& III**

CORRUPTED BY A GANGSTA I, II III, IV

BLINDED BY HIS LOVE

THE PRICE YOU PAY FOR LOVE

DOPE GIRL MAGIC I II

By **Destiny Skai**

WHEN A GOOD GIRL GOES BAD

By **Adrienne**

THE COST OF LOYALTY I II III

By Kweli

A GANGSTER'S REVENGE **I II III & IV**

THE BOSS MAN'S DAUGHTERS I II III IV V

A SAVAGE LOVE **I & II**

BAE BELONGS TO ME I II

A HUSTLER'S DECEIT I, II, III

WHAT BAD BITCHES DO I, II, III

SOUL OF A MONSTER I II III

KILL ZONE

A DOPE BOY'S QUEEN

By **Aryanna**

191

Adrian Dulan

A KINGPIN'S AMBITON
A KINGPIN'S AMBITION **II**
I MURDER FOR THE DOUGH
By **Ambitious**
TRUE SAVAGE I II III IV V VI
DOPE BOY MAGIC I, II, III
MIDNIGHT CARTEL I II
By **Chris Green**
A DOPEBOY'S PRAYER
By **Eddie "Wolf" Lee**
THE KING CARTEL **I, II & III**
By **Frank Gresham**
THESE NIGGAS AIN'T LOYAL **I, II & III**
By **Nikki Tee**
GANGSTA SHYT **I II &III**
By **CATO**
THE ULTIMATE BETRAYAL
By **Phoenix**
BOSS'N UP **I , II & III**
By **Royal Nicole**
I LOVE YOU TO DEATH
By Destiny J
I RIDE FOR MY HITTA
I STILL RIDE FOR MY HITTA
By **Misty Holt**
LOVE & CHASIN' PAPER
By **Qay Crockett**
TO DIE IN VAIN
SINS OF A HUSTLA
By **ASAD**

192

BROOKLYN HUSTLAZ
By **Boogsy Morina**
BROOKLYN ON LOCK I & II
By **Sonovia**
GANGSTA CITY
By **Teddy Duke**
A DRUG KING AND HIS DIAMOND I & II III
A DOPEMAN'S RICHES
HER MAN, MINE'S TOO I, II
CASH MONEY HO'S
By Nicole Goosby
TRAPHOUSE KING **I II & III**
KINGPIN KILLAZ I II III
STREET KINGS I II
PAID IN BLOOD **I II**
CARTEL KILLAZ I II III
DOPE GODS
By **Hood Rich**
LIPSTICK KILLAH **I, II, III**
CRIME OF PASSION I II & III
By **Mimi**
STEADY MOBBN' **I, II, III**
THE STREETS STAINED MY SOUL
By **Marcellus Allen**
WHO SHOT YA **I, II, III**
SON OF A DOPE FIEND
Renta
GORILLAZ IN THE BAY **I II III IV**
TEARS OF A GANGSTA I II
DE'KARI

Adrian Dulan

TRIGGADALE I II III
Elijah R. Freeman
GOD BLESS THE TRAPPERS I, II, III
THESE SCANDALOUS STREETS I, II, III
FEAR MY GANGSTA I, II, III IV
THESE STREETS DON'T LOVE NOBODY I, II
BURY ME A G I, II, III, IV, V
A GANGSTA'S EMPIRE I, II, III, IV
THE DOPEMAN'S BODYGAURD I II
Tranay Adams
THE STREETS ARE CALLING
Duquie Wilson
MARRIED TO A BOSS… I II III
By Destiny Skai & Chris Green
KINGZ OF THE GAME I II III IV
Playa Ray
SLAUGHTER GANG I II III
RUTHLESS HEART I II III
By Willie Slaughter
FUK SHYT
By Blakk Diamond
DON'T F#CK WITH MY HEART I II
By Linnea
ADDICTED TO THE DRAMA I II III
By Jamila
YAYO I II III
A SHOOTER'S AMBITION I II
By S. Allen
TRAP GOD
By Troublesome

194

Glocks on Satin Sheets 2

FOREVER GANGSTA

GLOCKS ON SATIN SHEETS I II

By Adrian Dulan

TOE TAGZ I II III

By Ah'Million

KINGPIN DREAMS I II

By Paper Boi Rari

CONFESSIONS OF A GANGSTA

By Nicholas Lock

I'M NOTHING WITHOUT HIS LOVE

By Monet Dragun

CAUGHT UP IN THE LIFE I II

By Robert Baptiste

NEW TO THE GAME I II III

By **Malik D. Rice**

LIFE OF A SAVAGE I II III

A GANGSTA'S QUR'AN

By **Romell Tukes**

LOYALTY AIN'T PROMISED

By Keith Williams

QUIET MONEY I II

THUG LIFE

By **Trai'Quan**

THE STREETS MADE ME I II

By **Larry D. Wright**

THE ULTIMATE SACRIFICE I, II, III, IV, V

KHADIFI

IF YOU CROSS ME ONCE

By **Anthony Fields**

THE LIFE OF A HOOD STAR

Adrian Dulan

By Ca$h & Rashia Wilson

BOOKS BY LDP'S CEO, CASH

TRUST IN NO MAN

TRUST IN NO MAN 2

TRUST IN NO MAN 3

BONDED BY BLOOD

SHORTY GOT A THUG

THUGS CRY

THUGS CRY 2

THUGS CRY 3

TRUST NO BITCH

TRUST NO BITCH 2

TRUST NO BITCH 3

TIL MY CASKET DROPS

RESTRAINING ORDER

RESTRAINING ORDER 2

IN LOVE WITH A CONVICT

LIFE OF A HOOD STAR

Coming Soon

BONDED BY BLOOD 2

BOW DOWN TO MY GANGSTA

Adrian Dulan

CPSIA information can be obtained
at www.ICGtesting.com
Printed in the USA
LVHW031913161220
674343LV00015B/1919